A Wounded Deer

Kneeling beside the doe, Val heard the bitterness in her father's voice. The gauze pad he was pressing against the wound quickly turned red with blood, and Val's eyes filled with tears.

Miss Maggie picked up one of the lanterns and held it out so Doc could see better. "I wish I could get my hands on whoever is responsible for this outrage," she muttered. "I'd show him a thing or two about sport! Better yet, I'd show him this poor, innocent creature. I can't imagine that even the most hard-hearted hunter would be able to ignore her suffering!"

Val glanced up at Toby. "Venison, huh?" she said.

Toby was silent.

ANIMAL INN

OH DEER!

Virginia Vail

AN
APPLE
PAPERBACK

SCHOLASTIC INC.
New York Toronto London Auckland Sydney

ISBN 0-590-42802-0

12 11 10 9 8 7 6 5 4 3 2   4 5/9

Printed in the U.S.A.   40
First Scholastic printing, December 1990

For Arnold, Waeshiea, Andrea, Hilary, Chad, Lois, Sherrie, Dana, and all the other fans of **ANIMAL INN** who have written such wonderful letters to me.

OH DEER!

Chapter 1

"Val, look out!"

Jill Dearborne's warning came too late. A snowball hit Valentine Taylor right between the shoulder blades.

"Bull's-eye!" a boy yelled. Then another snowball whizzed past Val, hitting her best friend on the arm.

"Snowball fight!" Val shouted. "Come on, Jill — let's get our revenge!"

The girls dropped their book bags and began scooping snow with their mittened hands. "That was Roger Henderson," Jill said. "He and Kenny Feldman have been following us ever since we left school."

Val grinned. "You think I didn't notice? I was just waiting for them to fire the first shot." She spun around and threw a snowball at one of the two figures running down the sidewalk behind them.

"You got him!" Jill cried happily.

"Who did I get?" Val asked, forming another

snowball. "It's snowing so hard I can't tell if it was Roger or Kenny."

"Who cares?" Jill sang out. She tossed a snowball at the boys and missed them both by a mile. "Rats!" she sighed. "From now on, what if I make the snowballs and you throw them? You're much better at it than I am."

Val's next pitch hit the other boy in the chest, and he let out a yelp. "That's Kenny," she said, giggling. "He sounds just like a dog! Quick, Jill — give me another one! Here comes Roger!"

"Hey, Taylor," Roger shouted, flinging a snowball at her as he ran past, "here's snow in your face!"

"No way!" Val shouted back. She ducked, then threw the snowball Jill handed her toward his back. It missed him, but hit someone else who was trudging through the snow a few paces ahead.

"*Roger Henderson!*" the person screeched. "How *dare* you!"

"It wasn't Roger, it was Val," Kenny hollered, dodging around Val and Jill and racing to catch up with his friend.

"*Val Taylor!*" The person in the bright pink parka whirled around and glared at Val. "How *dare* you!"

"Oh, terrific," Jill muttered. "Just what we needed — Lila Bascombe!"

Lila Bascombe was not one of Val's favorite people, or Jill's either. Lila considered herself a Very Important Person in the eighth grade at Alexander

Hamilton Junior High, although Val and Jill didn't share her opinion.

"Sorry about that, Lila," Val said, picking up her book bag and slinging it over her shoulder. "Jill and I were having a snowball fight with Roger and Kenny, and you just got in the way."

Lila scowled at her. "I could have been seriously *hurt*! What's the matter with you, anyway?"

"It was an accident, Lila," Jill said sweetly. "Just one of those things — you know how it is."

"I do *not*!" Lila scowled at Jill, too. "The two of you act like you're *three* years old instead of thirteen!"

"Like I said, I'm sorry." Val began walking next to Lila down Market Street, and Jill followed. "Honestly, I didn't mean to hit you. The boys started it, and we kept it up. I guess it was kind of silly, but we were having fun."

Lila sniffed. "Well, *some* people's idea of fun is pretty weird, if you ask me."

"We didn't," Jill put in. "Where are you going, Lila? This isn't the way you usually go home."

"For your information, I'm checking out the stores in Essex," Lila said, "so I can make up my Christmas list."

Val was impressed. "Gee, Lila, it's still only the last week in November. I haven't even started *planning* my Christmas shopping yet."

"Oh, I'm not doing that," Lila told her, brushing

the flying snow from her eyelashes. "I'm making a list of the things I *want* for Christmas. I check out all the stores and write down everything I'd like my parents and my sister to buy for me. It's mostly clothes, so I have to tell them exactly what designer and color, and the name of the store."

Val and Jill looked at each other. "When do you decide what you're going to buy for *them*?" Val asked.

"Later," Lila said. "Lauren's easy to shop for. But I have to wait until Mummy can drive me to Philadelphia to buy things for her and Daddy. The local stores don't carry the kind of things they like. Mummy only wears the most expensive French perfume, and Daddy just *loves* Italian silk ties. You wouldn't believe how much money I spend on my parents — almost as much as they spend on me." She dug into a pocket of her parka and pulled out a slip of paper. "My first stop is Brenda's Boutique. I'm meeting Kimberly and Courtney there so we can all make up our lists together."

"And I bet you all decide what you're going to buy for each other, right?" Jill asked.

"Of course," Lila replied. "I mean, it would be pretty pointless to give each other stuff we didn't really *want*. Then we'd just have to exchange everything."

"But if you know everything you're going to get,

you won't have any surprises," Val said. "Doesn't that kind of take the fun out of it?"

Lila gave her a disgusted look. "It is *not* fun getting presents you don't want. And I always get at least one of those from Great-aunt Maggie. What I'd really like this year is a fox fur jacket, but if I asked for one, she'd probably give me a subscription to the *Humane Society News!*"

Val shuddered. She wanted to be a veterinarian like her father, Dr. Theodore Taylor, and she loved animals so much that the thought of them being killed and skinned to make fur jackets for people like Lila Bascombe really upset her. Lila's great-aunt, Miss Maggie Rafferty, was a good friend of the Taylor family, and a good friend to the Essex Humane Society as well. When the local shelter had no room for more lost or abandoned animals, Miss Maggie always managed to find a place for them on her vast estate on the outskirts of town.

Val was about to defend the feisty old lady, but Jill poked her in the ribs. "Cool it, Val," she whispered. "If you get into an argument with Lila, you'll probably miss the bus, and there won't be another one for half an hour."

"You're right," Val agreed reluctantly. "I'm going to be late for work as it is." Val worked at her father's veterinary clinic, Animal Inn, three days a week after school and on Saturdays. Usually she rode her bike, but today there was too much snow.

The three girls had reached the corner of Market and Main Streets, and Lila paused for a moment. "I'm going to Brenda's Boutique now," she said. She scowled at Val. "And if you throw one more snowball at me, I'll never speak to you again!"

As she stomped off down Main Street, Val grinned at Jill. "Do you think she means it? Because if she does . . ." She pantomimed throwing an imaginary snowball.

"No such luck," Jill said, laughing. "It would take more than that to shut Lila up!"

Val peered down the street. "Oh, good! Here comes the bus. Maybe I won't be too late after all." She headed for the bus stop, calling over her shoulder, "See you tomorrow, Jill."

The bus lumbered over to the curb and slowed to a stop. Val climbed on board. "Hi, Mrs. Mc-Cracken," she said to the driver as she took off one mitten and dug in her pocket for some change. "Some snow we're having, isn't it?"

Mrs. McCracken smiled at her. "Sure is, Vallie. Early, too. I can't remember the last time it snowed so hard in November. Going to Animal Inn?"

"That's right." Val dropped her coins into the slot. "How's Sheba? Has she had her kittens yet?"

"Just last week." Mrs. McCracken steered the bus away from the curb down Main Street. "Five of 'em, and they're the cutest little things you ever saw.

Tell Doc I'll be bringing the whole family in for a checkup before Christmas."

"Great. I can't wait to see them!" Val said.

She made her way down the aisle. The bus wasn't very crowded, so she found a seat next to a window and pressed her nose to the glass. Many of the store windows were already decorated for Christmas. Garlands were strung high overhead across the street, and each lamppost bore a perky red bow.

Maybe it wasn't too soon to put up the decorations at Animal Inn, Val thought, settling back in her seat. If there weren't very many patients, she would ask her father if she and Toby Curran, Doc's other young assistant, could start doing it this afternoon. They'd decorate the waiting room first, and then the boarding kennel. And on Saturday, maybe they could help Donna Hartman decorate the pet grooming salon. . . .

"Hey, what's going on? Why aren't we moving?" one of the other passengers called to Mrs. McCracken.

Lost in her thoughts, Val hadn't noticed that the bus had left the town behind and was now standing still on York Road, less than half a mile from her stop.

"Beats me," the driver said. "Looks like there's some kind of tie-up ahead. Cars are bumper to bumper as far as I can see."

Val looked out her window again. There was no traffic at all coming in the opposite direction. Suddenly she heard a siren, and an ambulance sped by.

"Oh, dear," fretted an elderly woman across the aisle from Val. "There must have been an accident. I hope nobody was badly hurt."

"Accident or no accident, I'm supposed to be in Middletown at four o'clock," said a large, red-faced man. He strode down the aisle to Mrs. Mc-Cracken. "Can't you drive this thing along the shoulder and turn down a side road?"

She shook her head. "Sorry, sir. I have to stick to my route. Just be patient — I'm sure we'll be moving soon."

Val looked at her watch. It was a quarter to four, and Animal Inn closed at five. At this rate, she'd probably get there just in time to turn around and go home! Picking up her book bag, she stood up and walked down the aisle.

"Mrs. McCracken, my stop's not very far down the road," she said to the driver. "Could you let me out here? I can walk the rest of the way — it isn't snowing anymore."

Mrs. McCracken shrugged. "I don't see why not." She turned around and said loudly, "Anybody else want to get off? If Orchard Lane's your stop, you'll most likely make better time on foot."

"*I'm* going to *Middletown*," bellowed the red-faced man.

"I know," Mrs. McCracken said. When none of

the other passengers stood up, she smiled at Val. "I guess it's just you, Vallie. Take care now."

"Thanks, I will."

The door opened, and Val got out. An icy breeze stung her cheeks as she walked along the side of the road past the line of cars. The snow was only ankle-deep, so she made good time. In a few minutes she was approaching the scene of the accident. Several people had gotten out of their cars to see what was going on. Val tried not to look, but she couldn't help herself.

A brown sedan was angled across the road, obstructing both lanes. The ambulance and Essex's only police car were parked nearby, their lights flashing. As she came nearer, Val saw two paramedics helping the driver of the car. The man began to walk toward the ambulance, and she breathed a sigh of relief. If he could walk, he couldn't be too badly hurt, she thought. She was about to continue down the road when she noticed something strange. The brown sedan seemed to be the only car involved in the accident. Did that mean that it had hit a *person*? And if it had, why weren't the paramedics helping the victim?

Val went over to one of the onlookers, a man in a plaid lumberjacket. "Excuse me, sir," she said. "Do you know what happened? Is somebody else hurt?"

The man glanced at her and shrugged. "No. Just the guy in the car, and it looks like he's gonna be all right. But the deer's dead."

"The deer?" Val repeated. "The car hit a *deer*?"

"Sure did. An eight-point buck." The man shook his head. "I been hunting for years, and I never shot a buck that big. And this guy's just driving down the road, and the darned thing runs out in front of him. Some people have all the luck."

Val suddenly felt a little sick. "I don't imagine he feels very lucky right now," she managed to say. "And as for the deer — "

The man in the lumberjacket cut her off. "Too many of 'em around here these days. They're all over the place, damaging the crops, and running across the roads causing accidents like this one here. The driver of that car could have been killed. If you ask me, they oughta change the laws so there's no limit on how many deer a hunter can shoot. That would reduce the deer population in a hurry. Save lives, too. *Human* lives. They're the only ones that count."

Val felt even sicker. "Are you sure the deer's dead?" she asked. "Maybe it's just injured. My father's a veterinarian — his clinic, Animal Inn, isn't very far away — "

"Forget it," the man said, cutting her off again. "It's dead all right. Look over there — it's lying on the other side of the road."

Val refused to look. Without another word, she

began walking away, anger building with every step. The man's words kept echoing in her brain: "*Human* lives. They're the only ones that count." Doc always said that *all* life was valuable, and that killing was wrong. Val believed it with her whole heart. That was why she wanted to be a vet like her father. She wanted to *save* animals' lives, not end them!

Turning down Orchard Lane, she paid no attention to the beauty of the snow-etched branches arching above her head, or to the squirrels that scampered along them, chattering merrily. All she could think of was the eight-point buck lying dead by the side of York Road, and the man in the lumberjacket who thought it deserved its fate.

Chapter 2

Fifteen minutes later, Val flung open the door of Animal Inn's waiting room and stamped inside. Toby was sitting behind the desk where Pat Demp-wolf, Doc's receptionist, usually sat.

"About time you got here," Toby said, grinning. "I thought maybe you got snowed in or something. Pat left a while ago — she's baby-sitting for her little granddaughter tonight, so she asked Doc if she could leave early and he said okay."

Still too upset to speak, Val glanced around the waiting room. There were only three people there. A dark-haired young woman whose name Val didn't know was sitting on one of the benches with a cat carrier in her lap. Bald, heavy-set Hank Fowler, one of Doc's regular clients, took up most of another bench, his sorrowful-looking hound at his feet. The third person was Mrs. Pollock, the chairperson of the Essex Humane Society board. As thin as Mr. Fowler was fat, she was holding the leash of her shaggy mixed-breed, Chester. She smiled and nodded her curly gray head at Val.

Val tried to smile back. Then she headed for the door that led to the two treatment rooms and the rest of the clinic.

"Doc wants one of us to cover the desk while the other one gives the animals in the infirmary their medications," Toby said as she passed him.

Val didn't say anything. In the hall, she took off her down jacket, stuffed her knit cap into one of the pockets, and hung it in the closet. She knew that her thick, chestnut-brown hair was probably a mess, but she didn't care. All she could think about was the dead deer and her conversation with the awful man in the plaid jacket. Frowning, she came back into the reception area.

"Do you want to stay here or do you want to give out the medications?" she asked Toby.

He looked surprised at her sharp tone. "What's eating you, anyway?" he said. "You mad at me for some reason?"

Val sighed. "I'm not mad at you, Toby. But I'm mad, all right! On the way here, the bus got held up by an accident on York Road. A car hit and killed a deer, and then this man I started talking to said it was the deer's fault and there were too many of them around and they all ought to be *shot*!"

She didn't realize how loudly she had been speaking until Mr. Fowler said, "Well now, Vallie,

13

you gotta admit the guy has a point. There *are* too many deer in these parts, and they're not staying in the woods where they belong. This past fall a bunch of 'em came right into my backyard and ate all the vegetables in my garden. And my house isn't even in the country — it's right on the edge of town."

"The same thing happened to me," said the woman with the cat carrier. "They destroyed the flower garden that I'd worked so hard on all summer long! I used to think deer were so pretty and harmless until then. And I've heard that they carry Lyme disease. I don't want my children getting sick. Something really should be done about them."

Val didn't want to argue with her father's clients, but she couldn't just stand there and say nothing. "The reason the deer are coming out of the woods is that people are cutting down so many trees to make room for houses and shopping centers," she said as pleasantly as she could. "The forest is their home. If they can't live there, they have to go somewhere else."

"They certainly do!" said Mrs. Pollock. "Animals have rights just like people."

"Maybe so," said the other woman. "But if *people* destroyed my flower garden, I could call the police. Deer just do what they please. And besides, what's wrong with shopping centers? If you ask me, Essex could use a few more. We moved here less than a year ago, and where *we* come from . . ."

Mrs. Pollock, Mr. Fowler, and the cat-carrier woman started arguing with each other. Mr. Fowler's dog began growling at Mrs. Pollock's dog. Mrs. Pollock's dog growled back.

"You really started something here, you know that, Val?" Toby muttered.

"I didn't mean to," Val said softly. "I was just telling you why I was in a bad mood. It's not my fault that they were eavesdropping! But I'm glad that you agree with me."

"What do you mean?" Toby asked. "Agree with you about what?"

"About the fact that deer have rights the way people do, like Mrs. Pollock said. And that it isn't right to kill them."

"Now wait a minute!" Toby said. "I never said that."

"But you do believe it, don't you?" Val asked. "If you didn't believe that animals deserve the same consideration as people, you wouldn't be working here at Animal Inn, right?"

Toby squirmed in his chair and shuffled some papers on the reception desk.

"You do, don't you?" Val persisted.

"Well . . ." Toby avoided her eyes. "It's like this, Val. My dad's a dairy farmer. Our cows are very important to us, so we take real good care of them.

And the other animals that Doc treats — well, they're farm animals and pets. People care about them a lot. But deer . . ."

"What about deer?"

"Deer are *different*. They're *game*. I mean, if it wasn't okay to shoot them, there wouldn't be a deer-hunting season, right? The state of Pennsylvania wouldn't let people hunt them if they were an endangered species or anything."

"But deer *aren't* different!" Val cried. "They're animals, just like cows and horses and dogs! And they *will* be an endangered species if people keep shooting them and hitting them with cars!"

"Hitting them with cars is different from hunting them," Toby explained patiently. "Hunting is a sport. You go out there with your gun, and it's like, man against beast. I shot my first deer when I was eleven years old. Boy, was I proud when my mother served venison for dinner!"

Val stared at him as though he had suddenly grown horns and a forked tail.

"You're a *hunter*?" she gasped. "You actually go out into the woods and shoot those poor, defenseless deer? And then you *eat* them?"

"Hey, Val, cool it, okay?" Toby said. "I didn't tell you before because I knew you'd freak out . . ."

"*I am not freaking out!*" Val yelled. "I just can't believe it, that's all. I thought you were my friend! I thought you loved animals almost as much as I do!"

16

"Now wait a minute, Vallie," said Mr. Fowler. "Just because the boy's a hunter doesn't mean he doesn't care about animals. I'm a hunter, too, and I love old Dewey here like he was a member of the family." The hound, who was straining at his leash trying to get at Chester, let out a mournful howl.

Chester began to bark. Over the din, Mrs. Pollock shouted, "Consider this, Hank Fowler — what if somebody decided that *dogs* were game and it was legal to shoot and eat *them*? How would you feel about *that*?"

Mr. Fowler was getting angry. "That's just plain silly, Rebecca Pollock, and you know it! Dogs don't go around eating people's gardens and destroying farmers' crops. We're talking about *deer*, not dogs! Isn't that right, ma'am?" he said to the cat-carrier woman.

"Oh, dear — I guess we are," she said weakly. "But there must be some solution to the deer problem in Essex other than killing them."

"There is!" Val put in. "There are all sorts of things we could do, like building deer-proof fences and using natural repellents, and . . ."

"Too complicated," Mr. Fowler said. "And too expensive. What I say is, shoot 'em!"

By now Dewey was howling at the top of his lungs and Chester was barking nonstop. Just then, Doc came into the waiting room, holding a lop-eared Belgian hare in his arms. Terrified by all the noise,

17

the rabbit struggled wildly to get free, but Doc hung on to its fat, furry body.

"What on earth is going on?" Doc asked loudly. At the sound of his voice, Dewey stopped howling and slunk under the bench Mr. Fowler was sitting on. Chester stopped in midyelp and began wagging his tail.

Doc smiled. "That's better." He brought the frightened rabbit over to the woman with the cat carrier. "Bentley's going to be just fine, Mrs. Walters," he said. "Keep him on a high-fiber diet, and he won't have any more digestive problems."

Mrs. Walters took the rabbit and put him into the cat carrier. "Thank you, Dr. Taylor," she said. "Did you test him for Lyme disease? We've had a lot of deer on our property, and I've been so afraid that Bentley might have been infected."

"No symptoms at all," Doc assured her. "There hasn't been a single case reported in the entire county. Bentley's a perfectly healthy rabbit, aside from his tummy trouble." As Mrs. Walters put on her coat and hurried out with Bentley, he turned to Toby. "Who's next?"

Toby glanced at the appointment book. "Chester Pollock," he mumbled. "Time for his three-in-one shot."

Mrs. Pollock let go of Chester's leash, and he scampered over to Doc, leaping up and trying to lick his face.

"You're looking good, Chester," Doc said as he took the leash and led the happy mongrel to the door. "This won't take long, Rebecca. And then it will be Dewey's turn."

"Hey, Doc, mind if I ask you a question?" Mr. Fowler said.

Doc paused in the doorway. "Not at all. Shoot."

Val cringed. The word "shoot" wasn't the best one her father could have used under the circumstances.

"We were having a little discussion here right before you came in . . ." Mr. Fowler began.

" 'A little discussion'! Hah!" said Mrs. Pollock, glaring at the big, beefy man.

Mr. Fowler paid no attention to her. "We were talking about the deer problem here in Essex. You know what I mean — all those deer coming into people's backyards and running across the roads. One of them was hit by a car this very afternoon, according to Vallie. The driver could've been killed."

"The deer *was* killed," Val muttered.

"So what I want to know is, where do you stand? On the deer question, I mean," Mr. Fowler went on. "A bunch of us concerned citizens are going to have a meeting next Wednesday to decide what we're going to do about it. And it would sure help if the only vet in town was on our side. You *are* on our side, aren't you? Just because you take care of pets and farm animals doesn't mean you're one of those bleeding hearts like Rebecca here, right?"

"I am *not* . . ." Mrs. Pollock sputtered, but she was too angry to finish her sentence.

Doc rubbed his short, graying beard. "Well now, Hank," he said, "as you know, Rebecca and I both serve on the Humane Society board here in Essex, and we're both very concerned about animal rights."

"Unlike *some* people I could mention," Val said under her breath, scowling at Toby.

"And that means *all* animals," Doc went on. "Take a look at Chester for example."

Chester was sitting on the floor by Doc's feet, his long, pink tongue lolling out of his mouth.

"I see him. So what?" said Mr. Fowler.

"Chester has four legs and a tail. So do deer, if I'm not mistaken. But Chester doesn't have to worry about where his next meal is coming from, or where he's going to live when we humans destroy the forest that was his home. Neither does Dewey. Imagine how you'd feel if a car hit Dewey, Hank. I'll bet you'd be more concerned about your dog than about the driver. And I'll bet you'd bring Dewey right here to Animal Inn. We'd do the best we could for him, because he's a living creature that needed help. Deer are living creatures, too."

Mr. Fowler's face was getting red. "Now Doc, that's not the same thing, and you know it!"

"You know something, Hank? I don't believe I

do." Doc tugged on Chester's leash. "Come on, boy — time for your shots." He headed for the door to the treatment rooms with Chester trotting at his heels.

"I guess that means you won't be coming to our meeting," Mr. Fowler said.

Doc paused by the reception desk. "Oh, I'll be there, all right. Believe it or not, I agree with you that something needs to be done about the deer situation. I just don't agree that shooting more of them is the answer." He turned to Mrs. Pollock. "You plan on coming, too, don't you, Rebecca?"

"I most certainly do!" she said firmly. "And so do several other Humane Society members, including Miss Maggie Rafferty."

Mr. Fowler groaned. "Oh, no! That crazy old lady's a terror when it comes to animals! She'll probably suggest that we each *adopt* some of the darned critters!"

"Miss Maggie is *not* crazy!" Val burst out. "She loves animals just the way Dad and Mrs. Pollock and I do. She's the best friend those deer could ever have!"

"I know," Mr. Fowler said sadly. "This is sure going to be one interesting meeting."

Mrs. Pollock smiled. "It is indeed. I'm looking forward to it."

"So am I." Before Doc took Chester in for his shots he glanced down at Toby and Val. "And speak-

21

ing of animal rights, our patients in the infirmary have a right to receive their medications on schedule," he said. "I'd appreciate it if one of you would take care of that right now."

"I'll do it," Val said quickly. "I'm sure Toby would much rather stay here and talk to Mr. Fowler about what a great sport deer hunting is!"

Toby's large ears turned bright pink the way they always did when he got angry. "It *is* a great sport!" he replied. "And venison is delicious. You oughta try it some time — then maybe you'd stop being a vegetarian."

"*Oooh!*" Val stormed out of the room behind her father and Chester. "And to think Toby Curran used to be my friend!"

Chapter
3

As Doc and Val drove through the snowy streets an hour later on their way to the big stone house on Old Mill Road, Val was silent. The colored lights on the garlands that stretched across Main Street reminded her that she hadn't decorated Animal Inn as she had planned, but she didn't care. How could she be in a holiday mood when Toby, her second-best friend next to Jill, was a deer killer?

"I know what you're thinking," Doc said gently, turning the van onto George Street. "Or at least, I think I do. You're upset about Toby, aren't you?"

"*Upset?* I'm *furious!*" Val muttered. "I just can't believe that for all the time I've known him, he's been lying to me!"

"How has he been lying to you?" Doc asked. "Did the two of you ever talk about hunting before?"

"Well, no, but I just took it for granted that because we worked together taking care of animals, Toby felt the same way I do," she said. "And he

23

never said he didn't, so that's the same as lying, isn't it?''

"Not really." Doc turned onto Old Mill Road. "Knowing Toby, I imagine he didn't mention it because he wanted to keep the peace." Smiling, he glanced over at Val. "And knowing you, I can't blame him."

He pulled the van into the driveway, and Val unbuckled her seat belt. "It's not funny, Dad," she said. "It's like that movie we watched on TV the other night, the one about Dr. Jekyll and Mr. Hyde. Dr. Jekyll was so friendly and nice, but then he turned into a horrible monster!"

They got out of the van and began wading through the snow to the back of the house. Doc put an arm around Val's shoulders and gave her a hug. "Somehow I doubt that Toby will develop fangs and fur, don't you?"

"Dad! Be serious! You know what I mean," Val said, frowning.

"Yes, honey, I do. But try not to lose sight of the fact that a lot of perfectly nice people — people like our friend Toby — don't always see eye to eye with *other* perfectly nice people like you and me," Doc told her. "And we may never be able to change their way of looking at things. What we *can* do, though, when it comes to figuring out how to handle the deer problem here in Essex, is present some reasonable alternatives to shooting every deer on sight. That's what Mrs. Pollock, Miss Maggie, and I hope to do at that meeting next Wednesday."

"Can I come, too?" Val asked eagerly as she stamped the snow off her boots on the back porch. "I wouldn't say anything to embarrass you, honest. I bet Jill would come, too, and a lot of our friends. We could show people like Mr. Fowler that kids care about the deer as much as the old folks do."

Doc threw back his head and laughed. "On behalf of the other 'old folks' involved, I thank you for your offer, Vallie. But it's a school night and the meeting might run late, so I don't think it's going to be possible."

He opened the door, and he and Val came through the pantry into the warm, cozy kitchen. The two dogs, Jocko and Andy, dashed over to welcome them, barking happily. Val staggered back a step as Andy flung himself at her and planted his huge, furry paws on her chest.

"Hey, take it easy!" she cried, laughing. "I'm glad to see you, too. Just don't knock me over, okay?"

Andy galloped over to greet Doc, and Val bent down to pat bouncy little Jocko's black-and-white head.

"Stop right there!" said Mrs. Racer, the Taylors' housekeeper, holding up one hand like a traffic cop. Her voice was stern but her eyes were twinkling as she said, "Boots in the pantry, Vallie. You too, Doc. If one more person tracks melted snow across my clean floor, I quit!"

Val knew she was only teasing, but she pretended to be scared by Mrs. Racer's threat. "Yes, ma'am," she said, backing out of the kitchen.

Doc had already retreated to the pantry and was taking off his boots. "Sorry, Mrs. Racer," he said. "Us old folks tend to get kind of forgetful sometimes."

Val giggled. "Come on, Dad! I didn't mean *you* when I said that." She slipped out of her boots, hung up her jacket, and padded back into the kitchen in her stocking feet.

Doc hobbled after her. "Just hand me my cane and help me to my rocking chair," he cackled. "And then bring me my pipe and slippers."

Val was laughing so hard she could barely stand up. "Dad, cut that out! I'm sorry! You're *not* old — or at least, you're not *that* old."

Mrs. Racer shook her silver head. "Looks like the both of you got a case of the sillies. Isn't that right, Mrs. Sparks?"

"It certainly is," said the pretty, brown-haired woman sitting at the kitchen table. She smiled. "But I think Ted has the worse case!"

Val hadn't noticed her before. Now that she did, she wondered what Mrs. Sparks was doing there. Had Doc invited her and Sparky to supper again? Sparky was one of Val's little brother's best friends, and Catherine Sparks was a good friend of her father's. At least, Val hoped they were only friends, though Mrs. Racer had told her that she thought they were becoming something more.

"Oh, hi, Mrs. Sparks," she said.

"Catherine! What a pleasant surprise!" Doc was obviously delighted to see their visitor. He grinned sheepishly. "Excuse that little exhibition — I don't usually act like an idiot."

Mrs. Sparks laughed. "I thought you made a very convincing elderly gentleman. In case you're wondering why I'm here, I stopped by on my way home from work to pick up Philomena. I didn't want her walking home in all this snow. And then Mrs. Racer and I started exchanging holiday recipes, and I lost track of the time."

"I'm glad you did," Doc said, smiling warmly at her. "And since you're here, why don't you and Sparky — "

"Hi, Dad! Hi, Vallie!" Eight-year-old Teddy Taylor came charging into the kitchen, followed by Sparky. He threw his arms around Doc's waist in a gigantic hug.

"Mom, did Mrs. Racer give you her butterscotch brownie recipe, too?" Sparky asked her mother hopefully.

"No, just Christmas cookies," Mrs. Sparks said. "Sand tarts, and gingerbread, and pfeffernuesse."

Sparky wrinkled her nose. "Sounds yucky! I

don't want to make cookies with *sand* in them!"

"There's no sand in sand tarts, dummy," Teddy said. "Don't you know anything? They're called sand tarts because . . . Mrs. Racer, why are they called sand tarts?"

"Beats me," Mrs. Racer said. "Maybe it's because they're a pale golden color, like sand."

"What's that other thing you said, Mom? Fluffernutter?"

"*Pfeffernuesse,*" Mrs. Sparks repeated. "That's German for 'peppernuts.' And yes, they have pepper and nuts in them."

"*Double* yuck!" Sparky groaned. Then she glanced at Mrs. Racer. "If they're your recipes, I guess they gotta be good, 'cause you're the best cookie baker in the world, but they sure do sound weird."

"Philomena," Mrs. Sparks said with a sigh, "that was not very polite."

"It's all right," Mrs. Racer chuckled. "When you come to think of it, they do sound kinda peculiar."

"But they *taste* terrific," Val put in. "What recipes did you give Mrs. Racer?" she asked Mrs. Sparks.

"Only one — my grandmother's recipe for plum pudding," Sparky's mother replied. She grinned at Sparky. "And guess what, Philomena? There are no plums in plum pudding!"

"Do you know something else?" Doc said solemnly. "There's no ham in hamburger."

"There's no dogs in hot dogs, either!" Teddy added.

"And there's no straw in strawberries!" Sparky said between giggles. "Boy, is food funny!"

Just then a car horn honked in front of the house.

"That's m'son, Henry," Mrs. Racer said, taking off the apron she was wearing over her simple dark blue dress. She was a Mennonite, one of the "Plain People," and all her dresses were exactly alike, only in different colors. And she always wore a little white lawn cap perched on the back of her white hair. "Vallie, would you get my coat, please? And Teddy, my boots are right in the pantry."

"I can help, too. I'll tell Henry you're coming," Sparky said, and raced out the door to the hall.

"Say good night to Erin for me," Mrs. Racer told Val as she buttoned her coat. "Your sister's down in the basement, practicing her ballet dancing as usual. Well, I'm on my way. See you tomorrow, Doc, Vallie. 'Night, Mrs. Sparks."

As she hurried off, Mrs. Sparks gathered up her recipe cards and put them into her pocketbook. "It's time we were going, too," she said. "Mrs. Wilson has a meatloaf in the oven all ready for us, and I don't want it to dry out." Mrs. Wilson was her housekeeper, but according to Sparky, she wasn't nearly as nice as Mrs. Racer.

Doc helped Mrs. Sparks on with her coat. "I was about to ask the two of you to have supper with us, but in consideration of Mrs. Wilson's meatloaf, I won't," he said, much to Val's relief.

Sparky and Teddy came back into the kitchen. "Aw, Mom, we're not going already, are we?" Sparky said. "Teddy and me wanted to tell you about the neat snow fort we made today after school. Eric and Billy and us had a snowball fight with some of the other kids, and we *creamed* 'em!"

"You can tell me on the way home," Mrs. Sparks said. "Put on your jacket, honey."

"Oh, okay." Sparky trudged out with Jocko and Andy at her heels.

"It was a terrific snowball fight, Dad," Teddy told his father. "And Sparky's a pretty good snowball-thrower — for a girl."

"I heard that!" Sparky yelled from out in the hall. "I'm as good a snowball-thrower as you any day! And I'm lots better'n Eric!"

Mrs. Sparks sighed. "And to think I named my daughter Philomena because it sounded so delicate and feminine!" She picked up her purse and briefcase and started for the door.

"Oh, by the way, Catherine," Doc said, "there's going to be a meeting at town hall next Wednesday night to discuss the deer problem. I'll be going, and I was wondering if you'd like to go with me. I know you feel as strongly as I do that there are other ways to solve the problem than killing off the deer."

Mrs. Sparks frowned. "I most certainly do! Every time I hear hunters bragging about how many of the poor creatures they've shot, it makes my blood boil. By all means, count me in."

"Good." Doc smiled at her. "We can talk more about it on Saturday night when we go to the community concert."

As Doc and Mrs. Sparks left the kitchen, Val went over to the stove and peered inside the oven. But she didn't really see the casserole bubbling there. In her mind's eye, she was seeing the way her father had looked at Mrs. Sparks and the way she had looked at him. It gave her a funny feeling in her stomach, and though the casserole smelled delicious, suddenly she wasn't hungry anymore. Val had never seen Doc look at a woman like that, at least not in the three years since her mother had died in an automobile accident. And as if that wasn't bad enough, he'd asked Mrs. Sparks to go with him to the meeting, but he wouldn't let *her* go! She knew it was silly, but she felt hot tears stinging behind her eyelids.

"Vallie? You okay?" Teddy had come back into the room, and now he stood looking up at her, a worried expression on his usually cheerful face. "You look kinda sad, or mad, or something."

Val blinked. "Who me? You're imagining things, Teddy. I'm perfectly fine. Hey, isn't this your night to set the table?"

"It is not! I did it last night," Teddy told her. "It's Erin's turn. Want me to get her out of the basement?"

"No, that's okay. I'll tell her," Val said.

Teddy grinned. "Great! Then I can watch TV till it's time to eat." He trotted off into the living room, and Val went down the stairs to the basement.

She found her eleven-year-old sister sitting on a pile of cushions in a corner of the room Doc had made into a ballet studio for her. In her leotard and tights, and with her silvery-blonde hair in a neat ballerina knot, Erin looked exactly like their mother. Val looked at the many photographs of Mrs. Taylor that hung on the wall opposite the floor-to-ceiling mirrors behind the *barre*. Their mother had been a featured dancer with the Pennsylvania Ballet before she had married Doc, and now Erin was a star pupil at Miss Tamara's Ballet School.

Val was surprised to see that her sister was cuddling Cleveland, Val's big orange cat, in her lap. Usually, Erin wasn't very fond of Cleveland because he kept sneaking into her room, trying to figure out a way to attack her canary, Dandy.

"So *that's* where you've been," Val said to the cat. "I wondered why you didn't come to say hello when I came home."

Cleveland leaped out of Erin's lap and came over to Val. She picked him up and tickled him under the chin. "Mrs. Racer said you were practicing down here," she said to Erin. "What were you practicing — sitting?"

Erin shrugged. "I *was* going over a new variation Miss Tamara taught us today. But then I heard Mrs. Sparks come in, and I didn't feel like dancing anymore."

"I know what you mean." Val sank down onto the cushions next to Erin and flipped Cleveland over so he was lying on his back between her legs. She began rubbing his stomach, and Cleveland started to purr. "It's your turn to set the table."

"I know." Erin stretched out one slender leg and raised it over her head, her toes pointing to the ceiling.

The sisters sat in silence for a moment.

"She's gone now," Val said at last. "She and Sparky just went home."

"Good." Erin suddenly lowered her leg and tucked it under her. "I just *hate* it when she drops in like that. It's like she's a member of the family, and she's *not!*" She turned accusing blue eyes on Val. "Last spring, you told me that she and Daddy were just friends. But they've been dating for months now, and Mrs. Racer acts like she's something special. She even gave her the recipes for her special Christmas cookies!"

"Yeah." Val stopped rubbing Cleveland's tummy, but the cat still lay on his back, all four paws in the air. "And tonight, Dad asked her to go with him to a town meeting about the deer. I wanted to go, but he wouldn't let me."

"Do you think he's going to ask her to marry him?" Erin whispered, glancing at the photographs. "He couldn't! Mrs. Sparks is just a plain, ordinary lady who works in a lawyer's office! She couldn't possibly take Mommy's place."

"Nobody could." Val stood up, clutching Cleveland to her chest. "But if Dad decides that he wants to get married again, I'm sure he'll tell us. And he hasn't told us yet, so I guess that means he hasn't made up his mind." She looked down at her sister. "Are you going to set the table, or what?"

"I'm coming," Erin sighed. "Vallie?"

"What?"

"If he *does* tell us he wants to marry Mrs. Sparks, what are we going to do?"

Val rested her cheek on Cleveland's thick fur. "I don't know. Nothing, I guess. There's nothing we *can* do."

Erin frowned. "I don't believe that. Daddy loves us and he wants us to be happy. If he knew that we'd all be *miserable* if he got married again, I bet he wouldn't do it."

Cleveland was beginning to struggle, so Val put him down. "I don't think Teddy would be miserable. Sparky's one of his best friends, and he likes Mrs. Sparks, too. He probably wouldn't mind at all."

"Whose side are you on, anyway?" Erin asked irritably.

"What do you mean, whose side am I on?" Val followed Cleveland to the basement stairs. "You sound as if this was some kind of war — us against Mrs. Sparks."

Erin leaped to her feet. "Well, isn't it?"

Turning to face her sister, Val said quietly, "If we're against Mrs. Sparks, and Dad likes her so much that he's thinking of marrying her, then we're against Dad, too."

"Oh, Vallie, we're not!" Erin gazed up at a photograph of their mother in the ballet of *Cinderella*. "Remember what happened to her?"

Confused, Val said, "To Mom? You mean the accident?"

"No!" Erin cried. "None of us will ever forget that. I'm talking about Cinderella. After *her* mother died, her father got married again, and Cinderella's wicked stepmother was *horrible* to her!"

Val rolled her eyes. "Gimme a break, Erin! That's just a fairy tale. This is real life, and no matter how much I don't want Mrs. Sparks for a stepmother, I can't honestly think she'd be as bad as Cinderella's."

"Hello, down there!" From the top of the stairs, Doc's deep voice interrupted their conversation. "The casserole's done, I've made a salad, and Teddy and I are dying of hunger. So is Cleveland — he's sitting beside his bowl, yowling. How about getting a move on?''

"Coming, Dad," Val called.

"It may be just a fairy tale," Erin mumbled, "but I don't want a stepmother, wicked or not, and neither do you."

"No, I don't," Val agreed.

As she and Erin went slowly up the steps, Val felt unhappy and all mixed up. Half the people in town were mad at the other half, she and Toby were on opposite sides about the deer question, and now a battle was shaping up right here at home. Val didn't like it, not one bit.

Chapter
4

Val didn't go to Animal Inn the following day. Instead, she, Jill, and some of their friends picked up their sleds and toboggans after school and met at Beemer's Hill on the outskirts of town. Whizzing down the snow-covered slope with the icy wind whipping her cheeks, she was able to forget about all the things that were bothering her, at least for the moment.

On Friday, it started snowing again. As Val trudged through the flying flakes from the bus stop to the clinic, for the first time since she had started working there she wished she were somewhere else. The thought of spending the rest of the afternoon with her former friend, Toby the deer killer, made her cringe. She knew that Doc wouldn't have minded if she had said she wasn't coming today — he always worried that she spent too much time at Animal Inn and not enough time having fun with her friends. But Val loved her job — or she always had until today.

If Toby said *one word* about hunting, she knew she'd explode!

"Hello, Vallie. Merry Christmas!" Pat Dempwolf said cheerfully as Val came into the waiting room. "I know it's a little early, but I had some time on my hands, and I thought I'd put up the decorations. Doesn't it look nice?"

Val looked around. There were wreaths in all the windows, a tinsel garland around the bulletin board behind Pat's desk, and pictures of puppies and kittens wearing Santa suits were taped to the walls.

"It looks great, Pat," Val said, hiding her disappointment that she hadn't been able to help with the decorating. But she didn't feel very Christmassy anyway, so she supposed it didn't really matter.

"When are you puttin' up the tree?" asked the only other person in the waiting room. He was a small, middle-aged man holding a guinea pig in a box on his lap. The guinea pig whistled, and Val couldn't help smiling.

"Not till later, Mr. Geisler," Val said. She took off her mittens and stroked the little animal's sleek, reddish fur. "We always have a live tree, so we wait until about a week before Christmas to go cut it down. We get our own tree at the same time. What's wrong with Ginger?"

Mr. Geisler shook his head. "Durned if I know. Looks like she's got swollen glands. I sure hope it's nothin' serious."

From the look of Ginger's fat neck, Val decided that her problem was probably a strep infection. "I don't think it is," she told Mr. Geisler. "Dad will probably give her some antibiotics, and she'll be just fine."

"Toby's cleaning out the boarders' cages," Pat said. "I think Doc wants you to give him a hand."

Val paused on her way out of the reception area. "Oh. Isn't there anything else Dad would like me to do?"

Pat shrugged her plump shoulders. "Maybe. I guess you'd better ask him. He's in his office, writing up the last patient's chart."

Val went into the hall, hung up her down jacket, and put on a clean white lab coat. Then she peered into her father's office, but he was on the phone. He smiled and waved when he saw her, and Val waved back. With lagging steps, she headed for the boarding kennel.

Toby glanced at her as he dumped a pan of kitty litter into the plastic-lined garbage bin. "Hi," he said.

"Hi."

Val opened the cage next to the one Toby was cleaning and let out the fuzzy little Pomeranian inside. The dog frisked around, yapping merrily as Val took out all its toys, then picked up the mini-vacuum cleaner and began vacuuming the carpeted floor of the cage. Toby said something, but she paid no atttention.

"I *said* I already did that one," Toby yelled.

"You could have told me before I started," Val snapped. She turned off the vacuum cleaner and tossed the toys back into the cage. She picked up the Pomeranian, put him inside, and latched the door.

"I haven't done Tuptim Wentworth's yet," Toby told her.

Without a word, Val opened the Siamese's cage and took out Princess Tuptim. As she gathered up the cat's playthings, Toby said, "I guess you're still mad at me, huh?"

Val didn't answer. She just threw Tuptim's jingle ball across the room as hard as she could, and the Siamese dashed after it.

"You're acting really dumb, Val, you know that?" Toby said. "If you don't want to speak to me, that's okay. But it's not like I'm the only person in Essex who likes to hunt. What're you gonna do — stop talking to half the people in town?"

"I am *not* not speaking to you," Val replied sharply. "See? I just did." She began vacuuming Tuptim's cage. "And as for the rest of the hunters, it's not the same thing. *They* didn't pretend to care about animals, and then sneak out and shoot them behind my back!"

Toby's ears were getting red. "I wasn't pretending! I *do* care about animals. And I never snuck off behind your back! I just never mentioned it, that's all. Since when do I have to tell you everything I do?'' He opened the door of one of the cages. The minute he did, a black cocker spaniel ran out, heading directly for Princess Tuptim.

The Siamese let out an ear-splitting yowl and leaped up onto a windowsill. She hissed and spat, lashing out with her claws at the excited spaniel, who was jumping as high as he could, trying to reach her and barking frantically. The dogs and cats in the other cages began to bark and meow, too.

"Now see what you've done," Val shouted over the uproar. "If you *really* cared about animals, you wouldn't have let Jet out before I put Tuptim back in her cage! Mrs. Wentworth will have a fit if anything happens to her cat."

Toby raced over to the dog and grabbed his collar just as Tuptim swiped at him. She missed the spaniel and clawed Toby's arm instead.

"Ow!" Toby yelled. "I'm *bleeding!"* He glared at Val. "And if you say it's my own fault, I'll . . . I'll . . ."

Val glared back at him. "You'll what?"

"I'll think of something," Toby muttered. He shoved Jet back into his cage. "I've gotta take care of this scratch. You can finish the job by yourself!"

"That's fine by me," Val said as he stomped toward the door. "I can probably do it much faster alone, anyway!"

"Terrific," Toby called over his shoulder, " 'cause tomorrow you're going to be doing *every-*

thing by yourself. I won't be here — I'm going deer hunting with my dad!"

He slammed the door behind him, leaving Val more furious than ever.

For the rest of the afternoon, Val and Toby avoided each other. If Val was in the infirmary, Toby was at the reception desk; if Toby was feeding the boarders in the kennel, Val was visiting her horse, The Gray Ghost, in the barn; if Val was helping her father in one of the treatment rooms, Toby was building shelves for Donna Hartman in the pet-grooming salon.

Keeping out of Toby's way wasn't difficult, but it wasn't much fun, either, Val thought as she sat at the desk. There was nobody to talk to at all. Pat had left early again, and there were no patients waiting to see Doc. Either all the animals in Essex were in unusually good health, or their owners just didn't want to drive to Animal Inn on such a snowy day.

Val glanced up at the clock. Quarter to five — only fifteen more minutes, and then office hours would be over. She was beginning to tidy up the desk when the telephone rang. Val answered it.

"Good afternoon, Animal Inn."

"Margaret Rafferty here," said the brisk, no-nonsense voice at the other end. "Valentine, is that you?"

42

"Yes, Miss Maggie," Val replied. "Can I help you?"

"You certainly can! Or, more accurately, young Theodore can. Tell him to come out here right away. It's an emergency!"

"Oh, dear, what's wrong?" Val exclaimed. "Has something happened to Pedro?" Pedro was Miss Maggie's little burro. "Or Juliet, or Rupert, or Leander, or . . ."

"Pedro's fine, and so are all the dogs and cats," Miss Maggie cut in. "It's the deer. Somebody shot one of the deer I've been feeding right here on my very own property!"

Val gasped. "Oh, no!"

"It's not dead yet, but it will be if your father doesn't get here immediately. I'm going back out now with some blankets and a hot-water bottle so the poor creature doesn't freeze to death in the meantime," Miss Maggie went on. "Please tell young Theodore to *hurry*!"

She hung up, and so did Val. Then she raced into Doc's office. "Dad, emergency!" she cried. "Somebody shot a deer at Miss Maggie's place, and we have to get out there fast!"

Doc stood up and headed for the door. "Get my medical bag, Vallie. And get Toby, too. We'll need an extra pair of hands if we have to lift the deer into the van."

Val followed him down the hall to the coat closet. As they put on their coats, Val said, "I don't see what we need Toby for. I'm almost as tall as he is, and I'm strong, too."

Doc looked at her sharply. "I don't know what's going on between the two of you, but whatever it is can't be as important as saving an animal's life. Please do as I ask, Vallie."

Val shrugged. "Okay, I will. But don't be surprised if he doesn't want to come. He'll probably think the deer *deserved* to be shot!"

"So that's the problem is it?" Doc said, pulling on his boots. "You're still angry at him because he likes to hunt."

Val nodded.

"I know how you feel," Doc told her, "but somehow I doubt that Toby would refuse to help a wounded animal. Find him and tell him we need him, all right? I'll meet you at the van."

Val got Doc's medical bag from the first treatment room, then went in search of Toby. She found him in the infirmary, where he had just finished giving the patients their afternoon medications.

"There's an emergency," she said. "Dad wants me to ask you if you want to help us."

Toby grinned at her. "Hey, you're talking to me again! That's cool. Sure, I'll come." Then he stopped grinning. "What kind of emergency? Something real bad?"

"Yeah. One of the deer Miss Maggie had been feeding was shot. She's afraid it's going to die," Val said grimly. "You still want to come?"

"You mean because it's a deer?" Toby stared at her. "Gee, Val, I don't *hate* deer. What do you take me for? I said I'd come. What more do you want?"

"Hurry up, then," Val said. "Dad's waiting for us in the van."

Chapter 5

Nobody had much to say on the way to Miss Maggie's place. It was nearly dark, and snowflakes danced and swirled in the beams of the van's headlights. When they reached the Rafferty estate on the outskirts of town, Doc steered the van into the winding driveway that led to the house. Then he turned off onto a road leading to the fields behind Miss Maggie's garden. The road hadn't been plowed, so Doc had to drive very slowly and carefully.

"There she is!" Val cried as the headlights lit up a tall, angular figure ahead of them. The figure looked like an animated scarecrow, waving its arms and jumping up and down, but Val knew it was Miss Maggie in combat boots and an Army surplus parka.

"About time you got here!" Miss Maggie snapped after the van slowed to a stop and Doc rolled down the window. "What kept you? Well, get out! Get out! Your patient is right over there," she told Doc.

Doc, Val, and Toby climbed out of the van and slogged through the snow to a bundled shape covered with blankets. Miss Maggie had set kerosene lanterns on either side of the injured deer, and with the aid of the van's headlights they could see fairly well.

"I would've dragged her into the house, but she's too heavy and it's too far away," Miss Maggie continued. "She's been shot in the shoulder. Bleeding something fierce, too. Take a look at her, Theodore, and see what you can do."

Doc knelt in the snow and peeled back the blankets, revealing a frightened young doe. She struggled a little, alarmed by the sight of so many human faces, but she was too weak from loss of blood to do more than that. Val thought she had the most beautiful eyes she had ever seen, huge and dark and full of pain.

"Gosh," Toby whispered when he saw the bloodstained snow beneath her. "Looks like she's hurt bad."

Doc had taken off his gloves, and now he gently probed the area around the wound. "I think the bullet's still in there," he said. "We'll have to take her to Animal Inn where I can remove it. Vallie, get me some gauze and sterile pads. I'm going to try to stop the bleeding. Toby, bring the stretcher from the van. As soon as I've dressed the wound, we'll put her on it and carry her inside."

As Val and Toby hurried to carry out Doc's instructions, Miss Maggie hovered nearby, wringing her gloved hands. "Will she live?" she asked Doc anxiously.

"I think so," he replied. "Thanks to you, Miss Maggie, she has a fighting chance. If you hadn't found her and called us, this doe would certainly have become just another statistic."

He began to tend to the animal's wound. "Deer that are shot but not killed often suffer an agonizing and prolonged death. And not only deer, but other game animals as well. Hunters seldom bother to track down an injured animal — not much sport in that, I suppose."

Kneeling beside the doe, Val heard the bitterness in her father's voice. The gauze pad he was pressing against the wound quickly turned red with blood, and Val's eyes filled with tears.

Miss Maggie picked up one of the lanterns and held it out so Doc could see better. "I wish I could get my hands on whoever is responsible for this outrage," she muttered. "I'd show him a thing or two about sport! Better yet, I'd show him this poor, innocent creature. I can't imagine that even the most hard-hearted hunter would be able to ignore her suffering!"

Val glanced up at Toby. "Venison, huh?" she said.

Toby was silent.

Doc finished bandaging the deer's shoulder, and Val helped him to ease her onto the stretcher. Then Toby and Doc lifted the stretcher and carried it to the van. Val climbed in, crawling around the injured deer until she could rest its head in her lap. "You're going to be okay," she whispered as she stroked its slender neck. "My dad's the best vet in the world. Don't be frightened."

"Hop in, Miss Maggie," Doc said. "We'll drive you back to the house."

Miss Maggie joined Doc and Toby in the front seat, and they drove down the snowy lane to her big Victorian mansion.

"You'll keep me informed as to the animal's condition," Miss Maggie said as she got out of the van. "I expect a full report as soon as you've removed the bullet, Theodore."

"You'll get it," Doc promised. "We'll wait until you're safely inside."

Miss Maggie glared at him. "What do you think I am — some feeble old woman who can't go into her own house without supervision? Nobody shot *me* in the shoulder! Get going — I'll talk to you later."

"We're on our way," Doc said. "But would you do me a favor? Call my home and Toby's to let them know that we're going to be a little late."

"Will do."

Doc waited until the feisty old lady marched up the steps to the porch and into the house. Then he revved the motor and drove at top speed down the driveway to the main road and Animal Inn.

Half an hour later, Doc had removed the bullet from the doe's shoulder. Val and Toby settled her as comfortably as possible in the infirmary, with the help of Mike Strickler, who looked after the animals during the night and on the days the clinic was closed.

"Do't you worry none about this here deer," Mike said cheerfully. "I'll take real good care of her. I may be a hundred and fourteen, but I still got my wits about me!"

"I know you do, Mike," Val said, smiling. Mike was probably somewhere in his eighties, but he liked to pretend that he had passed the century mark long ago.

Serious now, Mike looked down at the doe and shook his head. "Poor little critter. I used to be a hunter once, y'know," he said to Toby and Val. "That was a long time ago — before I seen too many animals like this one. But most of 'em weren't as lucky as her. This one's gonna live. Lost my taste for deer meat back then, too . . ."

Toby shifted uncomfortably from one foot to the other. He had hardly said one word since they had set out for Miss Maggie's place.

Stroking the doe's head, Val said, "She'll sleep for awhile longer until the anesthesia wears off. Just keep an eye on her, Mike, and call us if she starts running a fever or anything."

Mike nodded. "Will do. Hey, Vallie, what're you gonna name her? It's more friendlylike if I can call her somethin' when I talk to her."

"You're right," Val said. "Let's see . . ." The wreath Pat had hung in the infirmary window caught her eye. It was made of plastic holly, with a big red bow. "How about Holly? That's a happy name, and it suits her somehow."

"Holly," Mike repeated thoughtfully. "Sounds good to me. Now you kids skedaddle. Me and Holly'll get along just fine."

"Okay. 'Night, Mike."

" 'Night," Toby mumbled as he followed Val out of the infirmary.

Doc was waiting for them in the hall, holding their coats. Val thought he looked tired. "Let's go," he said. "Toby, we'll take you home, of course. Thanks for giving us a hand. We couldn't have managed without you."

"No big deal," Toby said as he and Val put on their jackets. "You don't have to drive me. It's out of your way. I can take the bus."

"Don't be silly," Val said sharply. "You'd wait forever and you'd probably freeze to death."

Toby gave her a ghost of his usual grin. "Wouldn't that make you happy?"

Val jammed her woolen cap down over her ears.

"Maybe, but Dad would feel guilty about it."

The three of them trooped out of the clinic and piled into the van. Once again, nobody talked much on the way to the Currans'. When Doc pulled up in front of the house, he said, "Well, see you on Tuesday, Toby."

"Yeah," Val added. "You can tell us about all the deer you killed. I can hardly wait!"

" 'Night, Doc," Toby said, pointedly ignoring her as he got out. "Thanks for the lift."

Doc waited until the front door had closed behind Toby. Then he headed the van back toward town. "Aren't you being a little hard on him, Vallie?" he asked. "You have to admit that Toby worked as hard as you and I did to save that animal's life."

"He only did it because that's his job," Val said hotly. "If he really cared about Holly, he wouldn't be going out tomorrow to shoot more deer!"

Smiling slightly, Doc said, "Is Holly what you're calling the doe? It's a nice name — appropriate to the season, too. I keep forgetting that Christmas is only a few weeks away." He glanced over at Val. "But nobody seems to be in much of a holiday mood, not even you. I was kind of surprised that Pat put up the decorations without you, honey. You're usually Animal Inn's number one Christmas elf."

Val scrunched down in her seat, avoiding his eyes. "I was going to do it on Wednesday, but then there was the accident, and Toby and I got into that argument, and now Holly's been shot . . ." *And I'm afraid you're going to marry Mrs. Sparks*, she added silently.

"Holly's going to be all right, you know," Doc told her gently. "And Toby's partly responsible for that, don't forget. I think he still wants to be your friend."

"Well, I don't want to be *his* friend!" Val said. "And I am definitely not going to give him a Christmas present, so there!"

Doc sighed. "There's no need to make that decision right now. Wait a while. Maybe you'll change your mind."

"I will never, *ever* change my mind about giving a present to an animal killer," Val muttered. "As far as I'm concerned, Toby Curran simply doesn't exist!"

The minute Val and Doc arrived at Animal Inn on Saturday morning, they went into the infirmary to check on Holly. Mike hadn't called during the night, so Val assumed that the doe had no ill effects following her surgery. When she saw Holly, Val could tell that she was recovering nicely and, after a brief examination, Doc said she could be moved to the barn that housed the Large Animal Clinic. They half carried her there as Holly limped along between them, and placed her in a stall where she would be able to walk around if she felt up to it.

The Ghost watched with interest, whickering

softly at the sound of Val's voice, and stretching his dapple-gray neck out over the door of his stall to see what was going on.

"I bet you've never met a deer before, have you, Ghost?" Val said as she gave him his breakfast. "Deer are wild animals, and Holly is very timid. She's not used to being in an enclosed space like this. Try to make her feel at home, okay?" She kissed his velvety nose and rubbed him between the ears. "See you later. Maybe we can have a ride when I take my lunch break. The snow's pretty deep, but I think we can handle it."

"Coming Vallie?" Doc called from the doorway of the barn. "My first appointment is in about five minutes."

Val hurried to catch up with her father. She knew that this was going to be a very busy day, since Toby wouldn't be there to help.

But when Val and Doc entered Animal Inn, they found Toby seated behind the receptionist's desk. Val stared at him in astonishment.

"What are *you* doing here?" she squawked.

"What d'you mean, what am I doing here?" Toby replied, scowling at her. "I work here, re-member?"

"Yes, but — I mean, you said . . ." Val floundered.

Toby began shuffling papers on the desk and mumbled something Val couldn't quite hear.

"What?" she asked.

"I *said* I overslept," Toby said loudly. "You have to get up real early to go hunting, and I guess I forgot to set my alarm clock. And then when I got up, I couldn't find my socks."

"Your *socks*?" Val echoed.

"Yeah, my socks. It's real important to wear the right socks when you're hunting in the snow or else your toes freeze." Toby's ears were getting redder by the minute. "So by the time I found 'em, Dad and my brothers said they couldn't wait anymore, and they left without me. So I thought I might as well come to work since I didn't have anything better to do." .

Doc stroked his beard. Val could tell he was trying very hard not to smile. "Well, Toby, we're very glad to see you, aren't we, Val?"

"Yes, I guess so," Val said.

Toby looked at her for the first time. "Uh . . . when I came in a few minutes ago, I thought I'd check on Holly — see how she was doing, you know? And she wasn't there. She didn't — she's not. . . ?" Toby's voice trailed off.

Smiling broadly, Val said, "No, she didn't die. She's much better! Dad and I took her to the Large Animal Clinic and put her in a stall. Want to go out and say hello to her? I'll cover the desk while you're gone."

"I might just do that," Toby said. "Be back in

a minute!'' Without even stopping to put on his jacket, he raced out the door.

Val and Doc grinned at each other. ''You know something, Vallie?'' Doc said. ''It wouldn't surprise me if Toby 'forgot' to set his alarm on purpose.''

''Do you think maybe he's having second thoughts about hunting now that he's met Holly?'' Val asked eagerly.

''Could be. She's very *endeering*.''

Val groaned. ''Dad, that was *terrible*!''

''True.'' He tried to look ashamed of himself, but his eyes were twinkling.

The front door opened, letting in a blast of cold air and a snow-white poodle wearing little blue booties and a matching coat. At the other end of its leash was a woman all bundled up in a darker blue down coat. '' 'Morning, Doc. 'Morning, Vallie,'' she chirped. ''Here we are, right on time for Glendora's appointment. You'll be extra careful when you scale her teeth, won't you, Doc? Glendora has such sensitive gums.''

''Dad's always careful, Miss Flaherty,'' Val said. ''Just give us a minute to take off our coats, and we'll make sure that Glendora has the cleanest teeth in town!''

As she and her father went into the hallway to hang their jackets in the closet, Val felt happier than she had in days. She began whistling a little tune under her breath.

Doc smiled at her. "Sounds like you're getting into the holiday spirit at last. Isn't that 'Deck the halls with boughs of holly'?"

Val smiled too. "Yep. And you know what? Today I'm going to ask Toby to help me decorate the Large Animal Clinic. The Ghost and Holly deserve a little Christmas cheer!"

Chapter
6

Val was so pleased by Toby's change of heart that for the rest of the day she completely forgot about the other thing that was bothering her: her father and Mrs. Sparks.

But Erin hadn't. That evening after Doc left to pick up Sparky's mother for the community concert, she came into the living room where Val and Teddy were watching *The Black Stallion* on television. She sat down next to Val on the sofa and whispered, "Vallie, I have to talk to you."

"Can't it wait until the commercial?" Val said, her eyes riveted to the screen. "This is my favorite part."

Erin sighed. "*Every* part is your favorite part! You've seen this movie a million times. I need to talk to you *now*."

"Will you guys please shut up?" Teddy hollered. He, Jocko, and Andy were lying on the floor in front of the TV set. "I can't hear what they're saying."

"The black stallion isn't saying anything — he's just snorting," Erin pointed out. "Vallie, *please*! We have to talk about you know what."

Val blinked. "What's 'you know what'?"

"Dad and Mrs. Sparks!" Erin snapped.

A commercial for laundry detergent came onto the screen, and Teddy rolled over, peering at his sisters from under the visor of the Phillies baseball cap he always wore. "What about 'em?" he asked. "What's to talk about? Grown-ups are boring."

"Not when one of them might end up being our *stepmother*!" Erin said.

"You're outa your skull!" Teddy began wrestling with Jocko. "Dad's not going to get married again."

"I wouldn't be so sure about that," Erin said, frowning. "In ballet class today, my best friend Olivia told me that her parents think Mrs. Sparks is absolutely perfect for Daddy. And Mrs. Racer thinks so, too, doesn't she, Vallie?"

Snuggling Cleveland, who had leaped into her lap and was sitting there purring, Val said, "Well, she *likes* Mrs. Sparks . . ."

"From what Olivia says, everybody in town thinks that Daddy's going to marry her. But he mustn't! We can't let him!" Erin cried.

Teddy sat up. "You're crazy, Erin. If Dad married Mrs. Sparks, then Sparky would be my sister. I already have *enough* sisters — he wouldn't do a thing like that to me."

"But what if he did?" Erin persisted. "How would you feel about it?"

"I guess I wouldn't like it much," Teddy admitted. "I mean, Sparky's one of my best friends. But if she was my sister, she couldn't be my best friend anymore. You don't hang out and have snowball fights and stuff with your *sister*."

"Exactly," Erin said. "And not only that, if Sparky was living with us, she'd find out about Fuzzy-Wuzzy."

Teddy stared at her, horrified. "Omigosh! She'd laugh at me if she knew I sleep with that beat-up old teddy bear! And then she'd tell the rest of the gang, and *they'd* laugh, too. You're right, Erin. It'd be *awful* if Dad married Mrs. Sparks!"

"See, Vallie?" Erin said triumphantly. "I knew Teddy would be on our side. None of us wants another sister, and we certainly don't want a wicked stepmother!"

Teddy's eyes got even wider. "D'you think Mrs. Sparks would get wicked if she married Dad?"

"Oh, for heaven's sake!" Val sighed. "Of course she wouldn't. Erin's exaggerating." Before her sister could protest, she added, "Mrs. Sparks wouldn't be mean to us or anything. What Erin means is that she just wouldn't be Mom, that's all. I guess you don't remember Mom very well, do you, Teddy? You were only five when she died."

" 'Course I remember her," Teddy said. "She

was pretty and nice, and she smelled good — like flowers . . ." He lay back down on the floor, burying his face in Andy's shaggy beige fur. "I don't want to talk about her anymore," he mumbled. "It makes me sad."

"It makes *me* sad, too," Erin said. "And it makes me mad that Daddy doesn't seem to remember her at all!"

"That's not fair, Erin Taylor, and you know it!" Val cried. "It's not true, either. Of course Dad remembers Mom! What a terrible thing to say!"

Erin squirmed uncomfortably. "I'm sorry," she said. "But if he hasn't forgotten her, then why does he want to marry Mrs. Sparks?"

Val glanced down at her little brother. The commercial was over and the movie had begun again, but Teddy hadn't noticed. She couldn't see his face, but she thought maybe he was trying not to cry. "Hey, Teddy, look!" she said as brightly as she could. "The black stallion's racing. You don't want to miss what comes next, do you? And I have a great idea — during the next commercial, let's make some popcorn, okay? We can pretend we're at the movies in a real theater."

Teddy wiped his eyes on the sleeve of his sweatshirt and sat up. "Okay." His voice sounded a little husky. "With lots of melted butter."

As he turned his attention to the screen, Val whispered to Erin, "Will you please stop talking

61

about Dad and Mrs. Sparks? Like I told you before, if he's thinking about marrying her, he'll let us know. And if he does, we'll tell him how we feel about it."

"All right." Erin began watching the movie, too, but though Val stared at the television screen, she didn't see what was going on. Instead, she saw her mother's lovely, laughing face, and a younger, carefree Doc before he grew his beard and before his hair started turning gray. And then she saw her father smiling at Mrs. Sparks the way he had the other night. He'd looked younger then, too. He'd looked happy. If Mrs. Sparks could make him feel that way, did it matter how she, Erin, and Teddy felt? Val didn't know. She wished she could talk to somebody besides Erin about it, somebody who could help her figure out what to do. But who?

"Well now, Vallie, how did that big meeting go last night, the one about the deer?" Mrs. Racer asked as Val came into the kitchen on Thursday afternoon after school. The whole house smelled of cinnamon and ginger. Mrs. Racer had begun baking Christmas cookies, and she was rolling out a fresh batch of dough.

Val pinched off a little piece and popped it into her mouth. "Mmm — delicious!" she said. "According to what Dad told us this morning, it went pretty well. There were a lot of hunters there, and other people who agreed with them, but there were a lot of Humane Society people there, too. Dad said that when Miss Maggie told everybody about Holly being shot practically in her own backyard, even some of the hunters were shocked. All of them finally decided that instead of trying to increase the number of deer a hunter could kill, they'd form a committee to look into other ways of keeping the deer off people's property. I guess that means nothing's going to be done for awhile, but Dad seems to think it's a step in the right direction." She nibbled another piece of dough.

"Sounds good to me," Mrs. Racer said. "Want to help me cut out some gingerbread men, Vallie? Usually Erin does it, but she didn't want to today for some reason. She said somethin' about it not being the same since I gave Mrs. Sparks my special recipes. She went over to Olivia's house. And Teddy's outside somewhere."

"Sure. I'd love to help." Val rolled up her sleeves and picked up a cookie cutter. "I used to do this all the time with Mom when I was little."

Cleveland tried to jump up onto the counter, but Val pushed him away. "Oh no, you don't! Cats and cookies don't mix, as Mom used to say."

Mrs. Racer glanced at her. "You're thinking about your mom a lot lately, aren't you, Vallie? And so are Erin and Teddy."

Van shrugged. "Maybe." She began cutting out gingerbread men, lifting them with a spatula, and putting them on the baking sheet.

"I am, too," Mrs. Racer said, to Val's surprise. "I'm remembering how excited she used to get about Christmas — just like a little kid. Mrs. Sparks is kinda like that, you know?"

"Is she? I hadn't noticed." Val carefully placed another gingerbread man on the baking sheet. "There, this one's ready to go into the oven."

Mrs. Racer took out the batch that was already baked and replaced it with the new sheet. "Things change, Vallie," she said gently. "Life goes on. It's not good for people to hang onto the past, 'cause when they do, they miss out on the future, know what I mean?"

"You're talking about Dad and Mrs. Sparks, aren't you?" Val said. "You think he ought to marry her."

Mrs. Racer plopped another ball of dough onto the counter and began attacking it with the rolling pin. "I don't know if he *ought* to," she said. "But I think he *wants* to, and I think it would be good for him if he did. What do *you* think, Vallie?"

"I don't know *what* I think!" Val admitted. "He hasn't said anything about it, but Erin's sure that he's going to, and she and Teddy are dead set against it."

Putting the rolling pin aside, Mrs. Racer said, "A family needs a mother and a father. Doc needs

64

a wife. He loved your mother very much, Vallie, but you can't expect him to live alone for the rest of his life."

"But he's *not* alone! He has us!" Val cried. "We're perfectly fine just the way we are. If he marries Mrs. Sparks, everything will be different! And we don't *want* it to be different — we want things to stay the same!"

Mrs. Racer came around the counter and gave Val a hug. "Don't get all *ferdutzed*. Think about your pop. Think about what *he* wants and needs. I know how much you love him, and I know how much he loves you and Erin and Teddy. If you tell him you don't want him to get married again, he probably won't. But he won't be very happy, either. Think about it, Vallie. Think about it real hard."

"I *am* thinking about it," Val murmured. "It's almost the only thing I think about lately . . ." She sniffed the air. "Mrs. Racer, I think those cookies are burning!"

"Drat!" Mrs. Racer hurried over to the oven and opened the door. "They're not burned, just a little overdone," she said as she took out the tray. "If we put lots of icing on 'em, nobody'll notice. Let's finish this batch and then I'll get supper started."

"Why don't I roll and you cut for a change?" Val suggested.

"Fine by me. My arms were getting a little tired anyway." Instead of the man-shaped cutter, Mrs.

Racer picked up the lady. "Guess I'll use her this time. It wouldn't be right if none of those gingerbread men had a mate, now would it?"

Val stopped rolling and met the old woman's bright eyes. "I get the point," she said with a sigh. "But I still don't like the idea of Dad getting married again. I've got a lot more thinking to do."

As it turned out, Val didn't have much more thinking time. As soon as supper was over, Doc called a family conference. Val, Erin, Teddy, Cleveland, and the dogs settled themselves in the living room. Doc sat in his favorite chair next to the fireplace. He looked at each of his chidren in turn.

"There's something I want to discuss with you," he said. "You all know that I've been seeing a lot of Catherine — Mrs. Sparks — over the past few months . . ."

"Here it comes!" Erin whispered to Val, and Val whispered, "Ssshh!"

"What I want to say is . . ." Doc paused and rubbed his beard.

Teddy pulled the visor of his Phillies baseball cap down over his eyes. Erin clasped her hands tightly in her lap. Val folded her arms across her chest. For a moment, the only sound was the crackling of the fire.

"Well, no use beating around the bush," Doc said. "I've decided that I want Catherine to be my wife. I haven't asked her yet, but I'm pretty sure she'll say yes if I do. I need to know how all of you feel about it."

Erin poked Val in the ribs. "Tell him, Vallie," she murmured.

Val didn't say anything. She kept hearing what Mrs. Racer had said that afternoon — "Think about your pop. Think about what *he* wants and needs . . . think about it real hard."

"If you won't, I will," Erin said. She sat up very straight and looked her father right in the eye. "We don't want you to do it, Daddy. We don't want to have a stepmother!"

"I see." Doc turned to Teddy. "Is that right, Teddy? Is Erin speaking for you, too?"

Teddy scrunched down in his chair. "Yeah, I guess. If you get married to Mrs. Sparks, Sparky'll tell everybody about Fuzzy-Wuzzy, and they'll all laugh at me."

"Maybe she won't," Doc said gently. "Sparky's your friend. She won't stop being your friend just because her mother is married to your father. And friends don't tattle on each other, do they?"

Teddy thought about that for a moment. "I guess not, 'specially if I tell Sparky I'll break her face if she tells Billy or Eric that I sleep with that ol' bear."

Smiling, Doc said, "I doubt if that will be necessary. Any other objections?"

Teddy thought even longer. Finally he said, "I

guess not. If Sparky's gonna be living here, she'll have to do chores just like we do, right, Dad?"

Doc nodded.

"Then I won't have to walk the dogs as often, and I'll make Sparky help me clean the hamsters' cage. Maybe I can talk her into setting the table sometimes when it's my turn." Teddy looked much happier. "Besides, Mrs. Sparks makes the best spaghetti sauce in town! It's okay, Dad — you can marry her if you want to."

"Thank you, Teddy," Doc said solemnly. He turned to Val. "What about you, Vallie? Do you agree with your sister?"

"Yes — no — well, kind of," Val mumbled. "I mean, there's nothing wrong with Mrs. Sparks, and I guess you wouldn't want to marry her if you didn't care about her a lot, but . . . well, she's not Mom, that's all. Nobody could ever take Mom's place."

"You're right, Vallie. Nobody ever could, and Catherine doesn't intend to try. But she's very fond of all of you, and I think our two families could be very happy together."

"You love her, don't you?" Val asked.

"Yuck! Mushy stuff!" Teddy clapped his hands over his ears.

"Yes, honey, I do," Doc said.

"How *can* you?" Erin cried. "How can you just forget all about Mommy and love somebody else?" Her eyes were filled with tears, and one trickled down her cheek. "Mommy was *special* and Mrs. Sparks isn't special at all! She's just *ordinary*!"

Doc shook his head. "No, Erin, you're wrong. To me, she's very special indeed. And so are you, and Vallie, and Teddy, and Sparky. You're all special in different ways, and I love all of you very much."

Even though Teddy was pretending not to listen he heard that. "You love *Sparky*?" he squawked. "Gimme a break!"

Val shot him a look, and he wriggled off his chair and began wrestling with Jocko and Andy.

Doc continued talking to Erin. "I haven't forgotten your mother, baby. I'll never forget her. How could I, when the three of you are as much a part of her as you're part of me? But I don't think she would have wanted us to keep living in the past. Life goes on."

"That's what Mrs. Racer said." Val put her arm around Erin's shoulders. "And Mrs. Racer's always right." She took a deep breath. "If Dad wants to marry Mrs. Sparks, I think he ought to do it." The minute the words were out of her mouth, she wished she could take them back. She knew Erin would be very angry at her, and she was right.

Her sister leaped up from the sofa. "That's not what you said the last time we talked about it! You and Teddy were both on my side. It was three against one!"

"It still is," Teddy pointed out. "Only now Vallie, Dad, and me are the three, and *you're* the one."

Erin brushed the tears from her face, ignoring Doc's offer of the bandanna handkerchief he always kept in his hip pocket. "Nobody cares what I think," she wailed. "Nobody cares anything about me at all!" She ran out of the room and up the stairs. A moment later, Val heard her slam the door of her room behind her.

Doc stood up. "I'm going to see if I can calm your sister down," he said to Val and Teddy. "It may take a little time, but Erin will get used to the idea." He smiled at them both. "And so will you. Believe me, everything will work out for the best."

Val hoped that it would. But remembering Erin's tearstained face, she wasn't all that sure.

Chapter
7

"How are things going at home?" Jill asked on Monday after school. She and Val had taken the bus to the mall to do some Christmas shopping, and now they were wandering from store to store, peering into the windows at the merchandise displayed there. Carols blared from the loudspeakers, and happy shoppers thronged the concourse. Everybody seemed to be filled with holiday spirit — everybody but Val.

"Not too terrific," she said, pausing in front of Toy Town where animated elves were dancing jerkily around a pink plastic Christmas tree. "Ever since Thursday night, Erin's been acting just awful. It's like Teddy and I betrayed her or something. She hardly speaks to us, and she mopes and sulks all the time. I understand how she feels, but it's getting so that I want to shake her until her teeth rattle!"

"That's a shame," Jill sighed. "Mrs. Sparks is a really nice lady. My parents think it's neat that Doc's going to marry her, and so do I."

"Well, I'm not so sure *I* do," Val said. "I just can't get used to the idea of having two strange people living in our house."

Jill giggled. "They're not all that strange, Val. Sparky and Mrs. Sparks seem perfectly normal to me."

"You know what I mean. Mrs. Sparks will probably want to make all sorts of changes, and I like things exactly the way they are. So do Teddy and Erin." Val sighed. "But it's what Dad wants, and I want him to be happy, so I'm pretending that it's all right with me. Come on, Jill — let's go into Toy Town so I can buy a football for Teddy."

Jill followed her into the store and waited patiently while Val found a football she could afford. It was on sale, twenty percent off, and on impulse Val picked up another one. "I guess I might as well get one for Sparky, too," she muttered.

As they waited on the cashier's line, Jill said, "Are you going to buy a present for Sparky's mom?"

Val shrugged. "Maybe. Yeah, I suppose I'll have to. But not today. I'll get her a bottle of perfume or something next week."

"What kind of perfume does she wear?" Jill asked.

"How should I know?" Val replied irritably. "I don't know anything about her at all. But I *won't* get her lily of the valley. That's what my *real* mother always wore."

She paid for her purchases and took the big shopping bag the clerk handed her. "Are you about ready to go home?" she asked her friend. "You got stuff for your parents, and I've bought presents for Mrs. Racer, Sparky, Toby, and Teddy. Let's head for the bus stop, okay?"

"Sure. Whatever you say."

As they trudged in silence toward the exit, Val's heart was as heavy as the bags she carried. Usually she would have been eager to hurry home and show Erin the things she'd bought, and Erin would have helped her wrap them. But that was before everything had changed between them, and Val couldn't help thinking that it was all Mrs. Sparks's fault.

The one bright spot for Val these days was the time she spent at Animal Inn. While she was busy helping her father care for his patients, she was able to forget how different and uncomfortable everything was at home. Holly was improving rapidly, too, and that made Val feel much happier.

When she came into the Large Animal Clinic on Tuesday afternoon, she found Toby by the doe's stall.

"Hey, Val, look at this!" he said as she joined him. "I think Holly's beginning to know her name. Every time I call her, she turns around and looks at me." He leaned over the stall door. "Holly? Hi, Holly."

The deer turned her head and looked at him out

of huge brown eyes, flicking her tail.

"See? What did I tell you?" Toby said, grinning. He held out a piece of carrot on the palm of his hand, and Holly moved closer to him. She stretched out her slender neck and delicately took the carrot, then scampered into a corner of her stall to nibble the treat. "You *do* know your name, don't you, Holly?" Toby added, and the doe pricked up her ears.

"It looks like she does," Val said, smiling. "She's pretty smart. And to think that if Miss Maggie hadn't called us when she did, she'd probably be dead by now."

"Yeah . . ." Toby glanced at Val almost shyly. "Mom fixed venison steaks for dinner last night, but I couldn't eat any. Kinda lost my appetite when I thought about Holly here." He zipped up his jacket. "Guess I'd better get back to Animal Inn. You coming?"

"In a minute," Val said. "I haven't said hello to The Ghost yet. I don't want him to be jealous because we're paying so much attention to Holly."

She went over to her horse's stall. The Ghost stuck his head out, whuffling softly, and she put her arms around his dapple-gray neck. Instead of leaving, Toby followed her.

"Uh . . . Val?" he said. "Is everything okay? I mean, you're not still mad at me, are you?"

Val looked at him in surprise. "No, of course not. Why?"

"Well, you've been kinda quiet lately, like something's wrong only you don't want to talk about it."

She hadn't told him about Doc and Mrs. Sparks yet, and for some reason she didn't want to mention it now. Val took an apple out of the pocket of her jacket and offered it to The Ghost. As he munched it, she said, "I've got a lot on my mind, that's all. But it doesn't have anything to do with you, honest."

"Okay. I was just wondering," Toby said. He started walking toward the door when suddenly it flew open and two small figures bundled up in hooded parkas, mittens, and scarves dashed into the barn.

"Hi, Toby! How ya doin'?" said the brown parka.

"Yeah, how ya doin'?" the yellow parka echoed.

"Hey, it's Teddy and Sparky, right?" Toby said, laughing.

Val was even more surprised to see them than Toby was. "What are you guys doing here?" she asked. "And how did you get here? Did you take the bus?"

"Nope." The yellow parka pulled off its hood, revealing Sparky's stubby pigtails and round, rosy face. "Mom drove us. She had a dentist appointment so she took the afternoon off, and Teddy and me wanted to see Holly so she brought us out."

Teddy took off his hood, too. "Where's the deer, Vallie?" He ran over to The Ghost's stall and patted the horse's nose. "Hiya, Ghost. Long time no see."

Sparky trotted back to the door and yelled, "Hey, Mom, hurry up! Come meet Val's horse!" She grinned at Toby. "You know what, Toby? The Ghost's gonna be part of my family pretty soon!"

Toby stared down at her. "What are you talking about?"

"Didn't Vallie tell you?" Teddy shoved his mittens into the pockets of his parka. "Dad and Mrs. Sparks are gonna get married, and that means we're all gonna be one family. But Sparky's getting the best part of the deal. She gets Dad and Vallie and Erin and me and all our pets, and all *we* get is Sparky and her mom and their dumb old cat!"

"Charlie isn't a dumb old cat!" Sparky yelled, running over to him. "You take that back, Teddy Taylor!" Teddy gave one of her pigtails a playful tug, and she squealed, "*Mom!* Teddy's pulling my hair!"

"Teddy, take it easy," Mrs. Sparks said as she came into the barn. She was wearing a bright red down jacket, jeans, and boots. "And Philomena, quiet down. You'll scare the poor animals to death."

Toby glanced at Val, but she avoided his eyes. She could tell from the expression on his face that he'd guessed what was bothering her.

"Nice seeing you, Mrs. Sparks," Toby said, edging out the door. " 'Bye, kids. Val, I'll tell Doc that

76

your — uh — that Sparky and her mom and Teddy are here. See ya."

Teddy and Sparky had discovered Holly's stall, and now they were peering over the door at the doe. "She's so pretty," Sparky crooned. "She looks just like Santa's reindeer, only she doesn't have any antlers."

"*Girl* deers don't have antlers, dummy," Teddy said. "That's why only *boy* deers pull Santa's sleigh. Their antlers act like antennas and pick up solar vibrations. That's why they can fly."

Sparky threw him a disgusted look. "You've been watching *World Warriors* too much. Those aliens and androids have gone to your brain!"

While the two of them argued, Mrs. Sparks smiled at Val. "Aren't you going to introduce me to The Ghost?" she said. "I've heard so much about him that it hardly seems possible we've never met."

Val stroked her horse's neck. "Well, here he is. Ghost, this is Mrs. Sparks. Mrs. Sparks, this is The Ghost."

To her amazement, Mrs. Sparks reached up and put her arms around The Ghost's neck just the way Val had done. She rested her cheek against him and took a deep breath. "Mmm — nothing smells quite as good as a horse, does it, Val? When I was your age, I used to wonder why there wasn't a horse perfume. My best friend, Celia, was as horse-crazy as I was, and we decided we'd figure out a way to bottle it. We thought it would be wonderful to smell horsey all the time, not just after we'd been riding the horses we rented at the stable."

"You were crazy about horses when you were young?" Val asked. "I mean, younger?"

Mrs. Sparks laughed. "*Much* younger. I still am. When Philomena and I lived in York, I used to ride whenever I could get a baby-sitter. Is there any place in Essex where you can rent horses? In all the time we've been here, I haven't heard of one."

"No, there isn't." Then Val suddenly heard herself say, "If you'd like to ride The Ghost some time, I guess it would be all right. He doesn't see very well because of the cataracts in his eyes — that's why he isn't a champion jumper anymore. But he's perfectly okay for just riding. If you really know how to ride, I mean."

"Oh, I do," Mrs. Sparks said. "I'm not a champion either, but I've been riding since I was about twelve." She stood back and admired The Ghost. "I used to read about him in the papers. I'd consider it a privilege if you'd let me take him out some time. I never dreamed, even when I was a kid, that I'd ever ride a horse like this!"

The Ghost tossed his head and did a little dance, as though he knew he was being talked about. Val felt a smile tugging at the corners of her mouth. There was a warm feeling spreading through her, but she tried to ignore it.

"I guess maybe I'd let you," she said. "After all, you're going to be a member of the family, Mrs. Sparks."

Sparky's mother turned to her. She was almost exactly as tall as Val, who was proud of being five feet eight and still growing.

"Do you think you might be able to start calling me by my first name?" Mrs. Sparks asked gently. "I'd really like it if you and Teddy and Erin would call me Catherine. I'm not your mother, and I don't expect you to call me Mom the way Philomena does. But when Ted and I are married, I won't be Mrs. Sparks anymore. My name is Catherine. Will you try it, Val?"

Val shifted uncomfortably from foot to foot. She looked over at Teddy and Sparky. They had persuaded Holly to come close to them, and Sparky was patting the deer's head. *She's going to be my little sister*, Val thought. *She's not such a bad little kid. . . .*

Finally she said, "I'll try, but it's not going to be easy." Giving The Ghost one last pat, she headed for the deer's stall. "Let's go see Holly. She's getting better every day. Dad says that as soon as her wound has healed, we're going to take her to Wildlife Farm. She can stay there until the weather gets warmer and she's strong enough to be let loose in the woods."

"Aw, gee," Sparky said. "I thought you were going to keep her for another pet."

"That's wouldn't be right," Mrs. Sparks told her. "Holly's a wild animal; she needs to go back where she belongs with all the other deer. My, isn't she a pretty little thing!" She began stroking Holly, too. "You must be very proud of your father," she said to Val and Teddy. "His skill saved Holly's life."

"We're proud of him, all right," Teddy said. "He's the best vet there is!"

Mrs. Sparks smiled. "I know. I'm as proud of him as you are." Turning to Val, she added, "And I think it's wonderful that you're going to follow in your father's footsteps. 'Doctor Valentine Taylor' — it has a nice ring to it."

Now Val felt warm all over, and she felt her cheeks turning pink. "It does, doesn't it?" She smiled back at Mrs. Sparks. "Well, I'd better get to work. I'm really late today."

Laughing, Mrs. Sparks said, "And your boss is a terrible slave-driver, right? Don't worry about us. We'll be just fine. Maybe we'll drop in for a few minutes to say hello. See you later, Val."

"Yeah. See you later . . . Catherine." Still smiling, Val hurried out of the barn.

Chapter
8

"I'm not going! That's all there is to it!" Erin announced angrily on Sunday afternoon. "You can all go skating without me. I'm going to stay home and practice my solo for the Christmas assembly at school. That's a lot more important than hanging out with Sparky and her mother at McGregor's Pond. Besides, what if I fell and broke my leg or something? Then I wouldn't be able to dance for *months*."

Val rolled her eyes and plopped down on her sister's bed. "In the first place," she said, "you're a fantastic skater. You're not going to break anything. And in the second place, Dad suggested this skating party two days ago. Why didn't you tell him then that you didn't want to go?"

"Because you and Teddy thought it was such a great idea! Nobody asked me what *I* thought about it. Nobody even *cared*!" Erin stalked over to her canary's cage and poked a finger between the bars. Dandy hopped onto her finger, chirping merrily.

"Dad's going to be real upset if you don't come with us," Val said. "He wants . . ."

Erin pulled her finger out of the cage so abruptly that Dandy gave a little squawk and fluttered to his perch. "Daddy wants us all to be one big happy family, but that's not what *I* want! And I'm not going to go, so there!"

Val had been trying very hard to be patient and considerate. She counted to ten. She reminded herself how much Erin worshipped the memory of their mother. And then she leaped to her feet, ran over to Erin's bureau, and yanked the first heavy sweater she found out of the top drawer. Tossing it at her sister, she said through clenched teeth, "Put that on! And put on heavy socks! I'll get your skates. You're coming if I have to drag you by the hair!"

Erin stared at her. "What's the matter with you, Vallie? What do you care if I come or not?"

"I care," Val said grimly, "because Dad cares. And I love Dad very much and I want him to be happy. And he *won't* be happy if you keep acting this way! Think about somebody besides yourself for a change, okay?" She marched to the door and flung it open. "Be downstairs in ten minutes. That's when we're leaving to pick up Catherine and Sparky."

Ten minutes later, Erin came into the living room. Val and Teddy were waiting, and Val was holding her own skates and Erin's. Without a word,

Erin took the skates Val held out to her.

"This is gonna be fun," Teddy said. "Sparky and me are gonna race, and I bet I win!" He turned to Val. "Where's Dad? Let's get moving!"

"I think he's still on the phone," Val said. "He got a call a few minutes ago."

"Let's wait for him in the car." Teddy started for the front door, but before he reached it, Doc came out of the kitchen.

"Hold it, gang," he said. "I'm afraid there's been a change of plans."

"We're not going?" Erin asked hopefully.

"Not exactly. *I'm* not going, but you all are. Phil Landis's German shepherd is having convulsions, and I have to get over there right away. I phoned Catherine, and she'll drive you to McGregor's Pond. I'll meet you there after I've taken care of Helmut Landis."

"Poor Helmut!" Val cried. "Can I go with you? Maybe I could help."

Doc smiled at her. "No, Vallie. I'll handle it myself. But you can be a big help to Catherine by keeping an eye on Teddy and Sparky." He touched Erin's cheek. "You can help too, honey. You're the best skater in the family."

"I take after Mommy," Erin muttered. "She could skate as well as she danced. Mommy was good at *everything*. I bet Mrs. Sparks can't skate at all!"

Doc was on his way out the door so he didn't hear her. But Val did. "Erin, if you say *one more word* . . ." she hissed.

" 'Bye, Dad," Teddy yelled. "Hurry up and take care of that dog's revulsions so we can all skate together!"

"That's *convulsions*," Doc called back, laughing. "I'll hurry as fast as I can. See you later."

Teddy followed his father outside to wait for Mrs. Sparks on the front steps, and Val grabbed the dogs just in time to keep them from running out after him.

"I hope this isn't one of Helmut's really bad fits," she worried aloud. "He has epilepsy, you know."

Erin said nothing. She just stared out the living room window, a frown on her pretty face.

"What's the matter? Aren't you speaking to me?" Val asked, annoyed.

"I'm not supposed to say *one word*, remember?" Erin snapped.

Val sighed. "Oh, brother! This is going to be one fun skating party!"

A moment later, Teddy hollered, "They're here! C'mon, slowpokes — let's go!"

McGregor's Pond was about a mile outside of town on the old McGregor farm. Since it wasn't public property, only Mr. McGregor's special friends were allowed to skate there. Doc was one of his special friends, so the Taylors and their guests were always welcome. Unlike the lake in the town park where the ice was always crowded, there was usually nobody skating on the pond but Val and her family, and she loved it that way.

Mrs. Sparks slowed the car to a stop by the side of the dirt road that wound past the pond to Mr. McGregor's house and barn, and Teddy and Sparky immediately leaped out. Sparky's mother and Val got out next, but Erin stayed in the backseat.

"You're not going to just sit there the whole time, are you?" Val asked when Erin didn't budge.

Erin shrugged. "I'll get out when I'm good and ready," she said. "And I'm not ready yet."

"Suit yourself." Val stomped through the snow and joined the others. They were taking off their boots and lacing up their skates.

"*Double runners?*" Teddy squawked when he saw the skates Sparky was putting on. "Those are *baby* skates! I thought you said you were a dynamite skater!"

"I *am* a dynamite skater," Sparky said. "I'm a dynamite skater on double runners, aren't I, Mom?"

"Well . . ." Val could tell that Mrs. Sparks was trying not to smile. "Let's put it this way. You don't fall down nearly as much as you used to."

Teddy groaned. "Gimme a break! I thought we were gonna race!"

"Maybe Erin will race with you," Mrs. Sparks suggested. "Your father says she's very good. I bet she's fast, too."

"Yeah, she is. But Erin's no fun anymore. She doesn't want to do anything since . . ." Teddy caught Val's eye and didn't finish his sentence. "She's just no fun, that's all," he said instead.

"I'll race you, Teddy," Val said quickly. She stood up, brushed the snow off the back of her jeans, and tottered on her skate blades to the ice. "I'm ready whenever you are. *Now* who's a slowpoke?"

"Not me!" Teddy finished lacing up his skates and followed her. "Ready, set, *go!*"

"Don't go out into the middle of the pond," Sparky's mother called after them. "The ice might be thinner out there."

"We won't," Val said. She and Teddy took off, skimming over the ice close to shore. When they returned to their starting place, Val was ahead, but only by inches.

"No fair!" Teddy cried. "You've got longer legs than me! I would've won if you were a little shorter!"

"You know something, Teddy?" Val said, laughing, "you're right. Next year you'll probably beat me."

"I'll beat you next *week*," Teddy replied, but he was laughing, too.

Sparky and her mother were skating slowly,

hand in hand. Sparky was a little wobbly, but so far she hadn't fallen down. "Look at me," she shouted. "Aren't I doing good?"

"You're doing great!" Val shouted back. "Want to skate with me for a while?"

Sparky's round little face lit up with pleasure. "Oh, yeah!" She let go of her mother's hand and wobbled over to Val. Val grabbed her just before she fell, and Sparky looked up at her and grinned. "I'm gonna like having a big sister."

"*Two* big sisters," Val corrected. "Erin's going to be your big sister, too."

The brightness faded from Sparky's face. "I know. But she doesn't like me very much. She used to, but she doesn't anymore."

"Sure she does," Val told her, taking the little girl's mittened hand. "Erin's just . . ." She glanced over at the car and saw Erin still sitting inside. "She's *cold*, that's what's the matter. Erin's very delicate — the cold bothers her a lot."

Sparky shook her head. "I don't think so. I think it's me, and Mom. She doesn't want us to be part of your family."

Still holding Sparky's hand, Val glided across the ice. She didn't want to admit that Sparky was right, but she couldn't think of anything to say, so she just kept skating. Sparky was so intent on not falling down that she didn't seem to notice Val's silence.

Suddenly Sparky cried, "Hey, look at Mom! She's really good, isn't she?"

Val looked where Sparky was pointing. Mrs. Sparks, in her bright red down jacket, was swooping and swirling on the ice as gracefully as a ballerina. Teddy was trying to keep up with her, awkwardly copying her movements.

"She *is* good," Val said. "I didn't know your mother could skate that well."

"Mom's good at lots of things," Sparky told her proudly. "I guess that's why Doc wants to marry her. I think it's neat that they're going to be married. I used to miss my dad a lot after he and Mom got divorced and he moved to Texas, but he got married again, so I guess it's Mom's turn. And I know that Doc won't really be my dad, but he's awfully nice, and he acts like he likes me even if Erin doesn't."

Val squeezed her hand. "She does like you, Sparky. She just doesn't like the idea of having a stepmother, even one as nice as your mom. She'll get over being grumpy after a while — I hope."

"I hope so, too," Sparky said with a sigh. Then she looked over at the shore. "Oh, look, Vallie! Erin got out of the car and she's putting on her skates. D'you think she'd like to skate with us?"

"Maybe. Let's go see."

Val steered Sparky to the bank where Erin was sitting and glided to a stop, holding Sparky up. "Hi!" she said brightly. "It's about time you got out of that stuffy old car. Want to skate with Sparky and me?"

Erin concentrated on lacing up her skates. "Not really," she said. "I'm going to skate by myself."

Just then Teddy and Mrs. Sparks streaked across the pond and came to a stop, their blades creating a spray of ice crystals.

"Wanna race?" Teddy asked eagerly.

Erin shook her head.

"I'm looking forward to seeing you skate, Erin," Mrs. Sparks said. "I'll watch while I take a breather. Your brother's been running me ragged!" She sat down on a tree stump next to Erin. "How did you all learn to skate so well?"

Without hesitation, Erin said, "Our mother taught us. She was a wonderful skater, besides being a famous ballerina."

"Mom wasn't exactly famous, Erin," Val put in, and her sister glared at her.

"She was too. She danced all the leading roles in all the famous ballets! And she was beautiful, and a terrific cook, and the best mother in the whole world!"

Erin stood up and stepped onto the ice, sweeping past Sparky, Teddy, and Val. As she skimmed over the pond, Val thought that she looked like a little bluebird in her pale blue sweater and darker stretch pants. It was obvious that Erin had been watching Mrs. Sparks, because she did everything Mrs. Sparks had been doing, only better and more gracefully.

"What a show-off," Teddy muttered. "C'mon, Sparky. I guess it's my turn to drag you around for awhile."

He and Sparky skated off slowly and carefully, and Val turned to Sparky's mother. "I'm really sorry about the way Erin's been behaving," she said. "She's not usually like this."

Mrs. Sparks' shoulders slumped. "I know," she said wearily. "I can't blame Erin for resenting Philomena and me. But I keep on hoping I can make her understand that . . ." Her voice trailed off, and she stood up, shading her eyes with her hand. "Erin!" she called. "Please don't skate right out there in the middle — the ice may be thin!"

Erin kept on pirouetting in the center of the pond. "You can't tell me what to do," she called back. "You're not my mother! I'll skate wherever I want to!"

"Erin, stop being such a brat!" Val yelled. "Do what Catherine says!"

Twirling even faster, Erin shouted, "I will not! I don't have to listen to her or to you, either. I don't have to listen to anybody except Daddy!"

Suddenly there was a sharp cracking sound. Val gasped and clutched Mrs. Sparks's arm as Erin faltered, stumbled, then with a terrified shriek plunged through the ice into the frigid water beneath.

With Teddy's and Sparky's screams ringing in their ears, Val and Mrs. Sparks sped across the frozen pond to where Erin floundered, trying desperately to stay afloat by hanging onto the jagged ice around her.

"Be careful, Catherine," Val cried, grabbing hold of Mrs. Sparks' jacket. "Don't go any closer, or you'll fall in, too!"

Mrs. Sparks dropped to her knees, then lay face down on the ice. "Hang onto my feet," she commanded Val as she stretched her arms toward Erin. "And when I say 'pull,' *pull*!"

Val seized her ankles and braced herself. "It's okay, Erin," she shouted. "Take Catherine's hands! We're going to get you out! Don't be scared — *take her hands*!"

Gasping and sobbing, Erin did as she was told.

"Pull, Vallie! *Pull!*" Mrs. Sparks cried.

Val pulled with all her might. She was dimly aware of hands clutching her legs and pulling, too. Then she heard Teddy hollering, "Hang in there, Erin! We'll save you!"

It seemed like forever until Erin was finally lying on the ice. Her face was almost as white as the snow, and she was shivering uncontrollably. Mrs. Sparks gathered her into her arms and held her close. "Oh, Erin, thank heaven!" she whispered. "You're going to be all right, baby. You're going to be just fine!"

"Please . . ." Erin managed to say between chattering teeth, ". . . please . . . take me home. . . ."

Chapter
9

Mrs. Sparks, usually a cautious driver, broke all speed records on the way back to Old Mill Road. In the car, Val helped Erin struggle out of her cold, wet clothes until she was wearing only her undershirt and long johns. Then she wrapped her sister in a plaid woolen blanket Mrs. Sparks had taken out of the trunk. She hugged Erin, rubbing her arms and legs, but Erin continued to shiver and moan faintly. Her teeth chattered like castanets. Teddy and Sparky, their expressions solemn and worried, kept craning their necks to see how Erin was doing. For once, neither of them had anything to say.

When the car screeched to a stop in front of the Taylors' house, Val and Sparky's mother half carried Erin up the path to the front door. Once they were inside, Mrs. Sparks said, "Vallie, help me take her up to her room, then phone Dr. O'Toole. Tell him it's an emergency. And you'd better call Mr. Landis, too. If your father hasn't left yet, tell him what's happened, but try not to alarm him. Philomena, can you put the kettle on? Erin needs hot tea or broth as soon as possible. Teddy, find blankets, lots of them, and a heating pad if you have one."

Between them, Val and Mrs. Sparks helped Erin climb the stairs to her room. While Mrs. Sparks took off Erin's underthings and put her flannel nightgown on her, Val ran to the phone in the hall and called the doctor and Mr. Landis.

"Dr. O'Toole's coming right away," she said, racing back into her sister's room. "And Mr. Landis said that Dad just left a few minutes ago. When he doesn't see your car at the pond, he'll probably turn right around and come home."

Teddy brought blankets and the heating pad from the linen closet, and Mrs. Sparks plugged in the pad, tucked it under Erin, and piled the blankets on top of her.

"You'll be warm soon," she murmured, rubbing Erin's icy hands. "Don't worry about a thing — we'll take care of you."

"*Raaaow?*" said Cleveland from the doorway. Val ran over to her cat and scooped him up. She brought him over to Erin's bed and shoved him under the blankets.

"Cats are even better than heating pads when a person needs to be warmed up," she told Erin. "Their body temperature is much higher than ours. Snuggle up to him — until the heating pad kicks in, he'll be a good substitute."

Sparky came into the room, holding a steaming mug in both hands. "Here, Erin," she said. "This is camouflage tea. I couldn't find the regular stuff."

In spite of her concern for her sister, Val giggled. "It's *chamomile* tea, not camouflage," she said. "You're as bad as Teddy when it comes to long words!"

"I d-d-don't care what it's called, j-j-just as long as it's hot." Erin took the mug and sipped the tea. "It t-t-tastes good, Sparky. Thanks."

Mrs. Sparks got up from Erin's bed and hurried to the window. "Where's Doctor O'Toole? Why isn't he here?" she fretted.

"I only called him a few minutes ago," Val pointed out. "But I wish Dad would come home."

"S-s-so do I," Erin murmured between sips of tea. *"Ouch!"* she cried suddenly.

Val hurried over to her. "What's the matter? Is the tea too hot?"

"N-n-no — it's Cleveland. He just dug his claws into my t-t-tummy!"

"He does that sometimes," Val said. "Mrs. Racer calls it kneading bread. When a cat is happy and warm, he digs his claws into whatever's nearest. You almost never snuggle Cleveland, so you don't know about that."

Sparky had been standing beside her mother at the window. Now she yelled, "Dr. O'Toole's here! His car just pulled up behind Mom's!"

Teddy ran downstairs and opened the door before the doctor had a chance to ring the bell. Barely a minute later, he and Dr. O'Toole came into Erin's room.

"Oh, Jack, I'm so glad you're here!" Mrs. Sparks said. "Thanks for coming so quickly."

The stocky, blond young man smiled. "No problem, Catherine. Now let's take a look at the patient." He went over to Erin's bed and touched her cheek gently. "I understand you decided to go swimming a little late in the year," he teased, his eyes twinkling behind thick, horn-rimmed glasses.

He opened his medical bag, took out a thermometer, and put it between Erin's lips. Then he peeled back the layers of blankets.

"*Mmmrraaow?*" said Cleveland, blinking sleepily.

Dr. O'Toole grinned at Val. "You didn't tell me there were *two* patients, Vallie. Did Cleveland go ice skating, too?"

Teddy and Sparky giggled, and even Erin smiled a little.

"No," Val said. "He's just helping to keep Erin warm."

"Good idea." The doctor examined Erin briefly, then took the thermometer out of her mouth.

"Slightly subnormal, but not dangerously so," he said. "You're going to be perfectly fine, young lady," he told Erin. Turning to Mrs. Sparks, he added, "Keep giving her hot drinks, Catherine. Aside from that, there's nothing else Erin needs except rest." He smoothed the blankets over Erin and Cleveland and picked up his bag.

" 'Bye, Doctor O'Toole," Erin murmured drowsily.

" 'Bye, honey. Take it easy. You know something? You're a very lucky girl," the doctor said. "If your family hadn't been there to pull you out and take care of you the way they did, it might have been the end of you." He looked seriously at Val, Teddy, and Sparky. "Never, *ever* go skating by yourselves if you're not absolutely certain of the condition of the ice."

"We won't," Sparky and Teddy said together, and Val nodded.

Cheerful once more, Dr. O'Toole said, "And now if you'll all excuse me, I'll be on my way. I'd like to catch the rest of the football game I was watching on television when Val called."

"I'll see you to the door, Jack," Mrs. Sparks said as she and the doctor left the room.

"What channel is that football game on, Doctor O'Toole?" Teddy called after them.

"Channel eight," the doctor called back. "The score at half time was Eagles twelve, Lions seven."

"Cool! C'mon, Sparky, let's watch it in Dad's study!" Teddy and Sparky dashed out, leaving Val alone with Erin. She sat on the edge of the bed, careful not to squash Cleveland. "Want some more tea?" she asked.

Erin wrinkled her nose. "No — I don't like chamomile tea, but I didn't want to hurt Sparky's feelings so I didn't say anything. But I'd really love some nice hot chocolate."

"Okay," Val said. "Come to think of it, so would I. I'll make enough for all of us."

"Uh . . . Vallie, maybe you ought to let Mrs. Sparks do it," Erin suggested. "The last time you tried to make cocoa, it boiled over and made an awful mess, remember?"

Val grinned. "I guess you're right. But I'll put the marshmallows on top — there's no way I can foul *that* up!"

Erin smiled a little and burrowed deeper under the covers, her eyelids drooping. The only sounds in the room were the chirping of her canary, and Cleveland's muffled purrs.

Finally Val said softly, "Erin, I think you owe Catherine an apology. You were pretty rude to her today, you know. And you owe her thanks, too, for saving your life. We couldn't have done it without her . . . Erin? Are you listening to me?"

But Erin was fast asleep, or at least she appeared to be. Val gazed down at her sister, thinking that with her pale golden hair and rosy cheeks, Erin looked just like the Christmas angel the Taylors put on the top of their tree each year. Could someone who looked so angelic be playing possum? Val wondered. It seemed Erin's eyes were too tightly closed for a person who was really sleeping.

Val remembered reading somewhere that even if you were asleep, part of your brain could hear and remember things people said to you, so she whispered, "You're wrong about Catherine, Erin. She isn't ordinary at all. She's nice, and she's brave, too. She's not special the way Mom was, but she's a different kind of special. Give her a chance, okay?"

Erin's lashes fluttered slightly, but she didn't open her eyes. Val sighed. "I don't know if you can hear me or not," she said. "But if you can, just think about it." Then she kissed her sister's forehead, patted the lump that was Cleveland, and tiptoed out of the room, closing the door behind her.

Downstairs, Val found Mrs. Sparks in the kitchen. She was pouring milk into a saucepan, and the sugar canister and a box of cocoa were on the counter by the stove. "I thought I'd make some hot chocolate," she told Val. "I got the impression that Erin didn't much care for that chamomile tea, though she was very polite about it."

Val grinned. "You must have E.S.P.! That's ex-

actly what she asked for right before she fell asleep."
Or pretended to, she added silently. "I'll get the marshmallows."

Jocko and Andy followed her into the pantry, their tails wagging while they eyed the door of the cupboard where the pet food was kept. "Okay, okay, I get the point." She gave them each a dog biscuit, then found the bag of marshmallows and came back into the kitchen. The milk was heating on the stove, and Mrs. Sparks was sitting at the butcher-block table, resting her head on her folded arms.

"Catherine? Are you all right?" Val asked, concerned.

"Yes, I think so," Mrs. Sparks murmured. "I suddenly started feeling a little wobbly, so I thought I'd better sit down for a minute." She straightened up and tried to smile. "I'm pretty good in a crisis while it's going on, but when it's over, I tend to fall apart." Covering her face with her hands, she whispered, "Oh, Val, I haven't been so scared since Philomena was a year old and had a fever of a hundred and five! If you hadn't helped me pull Erin out, she might have drowned or frozen to death. And it was all my fault!"

Val stared at her. "What do you mean, it was your fault? You warned her about the ice, but she wouldn't listen. Erin can be awfully pigheaded sometimes."

Shaking her head, Mrs. Sparks said, "I should have been firmer with her, gone after her and brought her back when I saw where she was heading. But I didn't. I've been trying so hard to convince Erin that I won't be a wicked stepmother, I didn't want her to feel that I was bullying her, so I let her go."

"But you didn't know how thin the ice was," Val pointed out. "And you're the one who saved her. All I did was hang onto your feet. You're a hero, Catherine!"

"No, I'm not," Mrs. Sparks sighed. "Maybe Erin's right. Maybe it was a mistake, my agreeing to marry your father, if I can't take proper care of his children."

Val heard the faint creak of a board in the dining room floor outside the kitchen, but she paid no attention. "It wasn't a mistake," she said earnestly. "I have to admit I didn't like the idea much at first, but I've changed my mind. So has Teddy. And Erin will, too, just you wait and see."

Tears gathered in Mrs. Sparks's brown eyes and she brushed them away with the back of her hand. "I wish I could believe that," she said sadly. "I wish there were some way to prove to your sister that I love all of you very much, and that we can all be happy together."

"If you ask me, you *did* prove it this afternoon," Val told her. "Sooner or later, Erin's bound to understand. She's not pigheaded *all* the time."

Mrs. Sparks reached out and took her hand. "Thanks, Val," she said softly. "You've made me feel a lot better. I only hope things will work out for the best, for all our sakes . . . Oh, dear!" she cried, leaping to her feet. "The milk! It's boiling over!"

Before Val could get to the stove, Erin ran past her on slippered feet, Cleveland at her heels. "Honestly!" she said, turning off the gas and blowing on the bubbling foam. "I would've thought that between the two of you, you could manage to make a simple pot of cocoa!" Grabbing a pot holder, she lifted the saucepan off the burner and set it down on the counter. "It looks like even after Daddy and Mrs. Sparks get married, I'll still be the only *reliable* cook in the family."

Val and Mrs. Sparks glanced at each other in delighted surprise. Smiling, Mrs. Sparks said, "You know something, Erin? You may very well be right. Tell you what — if you're feeling up to it, suppose you give me a hand and we'll start all over." Val had a feeling she wasn't just talking about the cocoa.

"I feel fine," Erin said. "We'll need more milk and another pan. This one will have to soak for awhile."

"Are you sure you've had enough rest?" Val asked, taking the milk out of the refrigerator. "That wasn't much of a nap."

"I guess I wasn't as sleepy as I thought." Erin avoided her eyes as she poured the scorched milk down the drain. "Besides, it's hard to sleep when somebody keeps talking to you — or *about* you." Now she frowned at Val. "For your information, I am *not* pigheaded!"

Val grinned. "I thought I heard somebody in the dining room a few minutes ago! So you were eavesdropping, huh?" Erin opened her mouth, but before she could speak, Val said, "Okay, you weren't eavesdropping. You were sleepwalking, and you just happened to overhear what Catherine and I were saying."

Instead of answering, Erin turned to Mrs. Sparks. "We'd better make a really big batch this time, Catherine. Daddy's probably on his way home by now, and he's very fond of hot chocolate."

"I know." Mrs. Sparks put her hands on Erin's shoulders and looked down at her tenderly. "But there are a lot of things I *don't* know about your father, so Sparky and I are going to depend on you, Val, and Teddy to help us learn. Will you do that, Erin?"

After a moment, Erin nodded. "I'll try." Suddenly she smiled. "Hey, that's the first time I ever heard you call Sparky Sparky."

Mrs. Sparks laughed a little shakily. "Well, it's the first time I ever heard you call *me* Catherine.

Do you think you could keep on doing it?"

"I'll try," Erin said again. Her smile faded. Very solemnly she added, "It wasn't your fault that I fell through the ice, Catherine. I was angry, and I was showing off, and I was . . ."

"Being pigheaded?" Val suggested.

To her surprise, Erin murmured, "Yes, I guess I was." She hung her head. "I'm sorry. Thank you for rescuing me, and for taking such good care of me. And don't change your mind about marrying Daddy. All things considered, he could do a lot worse."

Val groaned. "Oh, terrific!"

But Mrs. Sparks just laughed and gave Erin a hug. "It's perfectly all right," she told Val, resting her cheek on the top of Erin's silvery-blonde head. "That's probably the nicest thing anyone ever said to me!"

Doc came home a short while later, full of apologies for missing the skating party because Helmut's seizure had taken longer than usual to control. Teddy and Sparky came pounding into the kitchen, and everyone began talking at once, telling him what had happened at McGregor's Pond.

"Catherine saved my life, Daddy," Erin finished by saying. "She really *is* a special person, like you and Vallie said."

Doc put one arm around her and the other

around Mrs. Sparks. His voice was husky as he said, "She is indeed."

The holiday feeling Val had been missing came flooding back. She was sure that this was going to be the Taylors' merriest Christmas in three whole years.

Chapter 10

Christmas was only nine days away, and suddenly it seemed to Val that there would never be enough time to get everything done. There were cards to send and presents to buy and parties to go to, in addition to school and her job at Animal Inn.

After school on Monday, she met Erin, Teddy, and Sparky at Fishel's Pet Emporium, where they put their heads together and decided on gifts for their animal friends. The cats were easy — catnip mice for Cleveland and Charlie. Sparky and Teddy pooled their allowances to buy two rawhide bones for Andy and Jocko, and Erin selected a mirror in a pink plastic frame for Dandy, "so he'll think there's another bird in his cage and he won't be lonely."

They bought a box of treats for Teddy's hamsters. After much deliberation, Val decided on a bright blue nylon halter for The Ghost to replace his worn-out leather one.

"What can we give Holly?" Sparky asked. "I

know she's not really a pet, but she deserves a present anyway.''

"The best present we could give her would be her freedom," Val said, "but since we can't do that until she's completely healed, I think we should give her a bunch of carrots. She likes carrots better than anything else.''

On Tuesday and Wednesday, Val worked at Animal Inn, and on Thursday, she and Jill went to the mall again, where she bought presents for Mike Strickler, Pat, Erin, Doc, and Catherine. It was difficult choosing the right gift for Catherine. Val finally decided on a silk scarf with a design of bridles, stirrups, and horses' heads because she knew that Catherine loved horses as much as she did.

"I'm glad you changed your mind about Sparky's mom,'' Jill said as Val tucked the scarf into her shopping bag. ''But I thought you were going to buy her perfume.''

"That was before I really knew her," Val replied. Remembering what Catherine had said about wanting to bottle horse perfume, she grinned. ''Nobody makes the kind of scent she'd like!''

"Are you coming to Miss Maggie's Christmas party on Saturday?'' Jill asked.

"We sure are! Dad and Catherine haven't told anybody yet that they're getting married, so they're going to announce their engagement then.''

"Terrific! I can hardly wait. Miss Maggie's party

is always wonderful, but this year it's going to be even better. Oh, Val, I'm so happy for you!"

Smiling, Val said, "So am I!"

On Saturday, Doc closed the clinic at noon, leaving Mike in charge.

"Gonna get your tree?" the old man asked. When Val said they were, he folded his arms and nodded. " 'Bout time you got around to it, what with Christmas only three days away. You're gonna get one for the clinic too, ain't you?"

"Of course we are," Val said, laughing. "We always do. Did you think we'd forget?"

"Well, I was kind of wonderin'. For a while there, you were walkin' around with a face a mile long, Vallie, like you didn't even know Christmas was comin'."

"You're right — I was. But everything's fine now. We're going to put up both trees and decorate them tomorrow. And since it's so late, Dad says we can leave them up for the whole twelve days of Christmas! We'll see you at Miss Maggie's party later, okay?"

Mike shrugged. "I guess so. Durned nuisance if you ask me, gettin' all gussied up in my one good suit, but I'll be there. I just hope nothin' goes wrong with the boarders, or The Ghost and Holly while I'm gone."

"Pat's son-in-law said he'd keep an eye on things

until you get back," Doc said. "If there's a problem, he can call us at Miss Maggie's. Come on, Vallie. Erin, Teddy, Sparky, and Catherine will be wondering where we are. I said we'd pick them up around one o'clock, and it's past that now."

" 'Bye, Mike," Val said as they went out the door. "See you at Miss Maggie's."

On the way out to Shumaker's Tree Farm, Teddy and Sparky bounced up and down on the back seat of the van, chanting, "Three days to Christmas! Three days to Christmas!" until Doc begged them to stop. Then Catherine, Erin, and Val began singing "Jingle Bells," and Doc, Sparky, and Teddy joined in. They were still singing as they marched through the snow beneath the bright blue December sky, searching for the perfect trees for Doc to cut down. After much debate, they settled on a tall blue spruce for the Taylors' house, a smaller one for Catherine and Sparky, and a little Douglas fir for Animal Inn.

"Next year you'll only have to chop down *two* trees, Doc," Sparky said, " 'cause Mom and me will be living at your house. I like your house much better than ours, don't you, Mom?"

"Yes, I do," Catherine replied with a smile. "But the very best thing about it is the people who live there!"

"And the dogs and the cat and the hamsters and the canary and — " Sparky broke off with a squeak when Teddy hit her with a snowball.

"Teddy, behave yourself," Doc said. "There's no time for a snowball fight now. We still have to get greens and wreaths, pay for everything, and get back to town in time to get 'all gussied up,' as Mike says, for Miss Maggie's party. It starts at five, and we don't want to be late."

"We sure don't!" Teddy agreed. "Race you to the van, Sparky!"

Everybody helped Doc tie the trees to the roof of the van, then climbed inside, their arms filled with fragrant pine and balsam. As they drove down the snowy lane to the main road that led to Essex, singing "The Twelve Days of Christmas" at the top of their lungs, Val remembered other tree-cutting expeditions when her mother had sat next to Doc where Catherine was sitting now. But the memory didn't make her sad. Those had been happy times, and this was a happy time, too. Meeting Erin's eyes over the bundles of greens they both held, she smiled and Erin smiled back.

". . . and a par — tri — idge in a pear tree!" they sang.

By six o'clock that evening, Miss Maggie's annual Christmas party was in full swing. It seemed to Val that everybody in Essex was there, and they were all having a wonderful time. Candles in silver candelabra cast a warm, flickering light on smiling faces, and every window and doorway was draped with boughs of fir and garlands of pine. Crystal bowls of holly and scarlet poinsettias were everywhere.

Someone was playing Christmas carols on the grand piano in the huge living room. Edging her way through the crowd, Val saw that it was the mayor, and Mrs. Pollock was turning the pages of the music for him. People were gathered around them singing, while others circled the lace-covered table in the dining room, helping themselves to the delicious buffet. Still others, Teddy, Sparky, and Erin among them, admired the enormous Christmas tree that sparkled and glittered with hundreds of antique ornaments. The many dogs of all shapes and sizes that the old lady had adopted over the years weaved between the guests' legs, gobbling the tidbits people kept offering them. Miss Maggie's cats were nowhere in sight, though Val had seen one or two of them lurking under the furniture when she and her family had taken their coats and boots upstairs to one of the bedrooms.

Every year, Val was amazed at the way Miss Maggie managed to transform her usually cluttered, slightly shabby mansion into such a gracious, elegant setting for her holiday party. And the most amazing transformation of all was Miss Maggie herself. Instead of the khaki pants, workman's shirt, and sturdy boots she normally wore, she always appeared in some exotic outfit. Tonight, she was dressed in a maroon caftan with tiny brass bells attached to the flowing sleeves. The bells tinkled as she moved among her guests, greeting each one and making sure that no one felt uncomfortable or left out. Now she was talking to Mrs. Racer, her son Henry, Mr. and Mrs. Bascombe, and Lila. Val could hardly imagine a more unlikely group, but they all seemed to be enjoying themselves enormously, even Lila.

After chatting with Jill and her parents, wishing Pat Dempwolf and Mike a merry Christmas, and waving at Doc and Catherine, who were standing by the fireplace talking to Donna and Jim Hartman, Val headed for the sun porch. It was very warm in the living room, and she needed a breath of fresh air.

She was surprised to find Toby there. He was sitting in one of the wicker armchairs, wolfing down turkey, ham, and assorted salads. In his tweed jacket, chinos, shirt and tie, he looked very different from the Toby Val saw every day at Animal Inn.

Apparently he thought Val looked very different, too, because his eyes widened when he saw her.

"Gee, Val, I've never seen you in a dress before," he said. "You look — like a *girl*."

"That's because I *am* a girl, silly!" she retorted, smoothing down the skirt of her brown velvet jumper. Erin had insisted that she wear it and her cream-colored, lace-trimmed blouse. She had helped Val style her hair, too, tying it back at the nape of her neck with a matching brown velvet ribbon. "You don't look so bad yourself."

"Thanks." Toby swallowed a mouthful of potato salad. "Great party, huh? Terrific food. How come you're not eating? There's lots of vegetables and stuff."

"I know. I'm just not very hungry." Val sat down in another chair.

Toby put his empty plate down on the floor, and one of Miss Maggie's dogs dashed over and began licking it. "Uh . . . Val, I guess it's none of my business, but — well, are you still upset about your dad marrying Mrs. Sparks?" he mumbled. "Because if you are, you shouldn't be. I mean how bad could it be?"

Val smiled. "It won't be bad at all. In fact, it's going to be just fine!"

Toby blinked in surprise. "It will? Hey, that's neat." Then he grinned at her. "If everything's okay, I guess you don't need anything to cheer you up, right? I brought your Christmas gift tonight in case you were feeling low, but if you're not . . ."

"If I'm not, you're not going to give it to me?" Val asked, laughing.

"Well, since I wrapped it and everything . . ." Toby reached behind him. He brought out a small, lumpy package, and handed it to Val.

"Thank you, Toby." She suddenly felt shy. "Dad's going to drive me to your place tomorrow so I can give you your present. I'm sorry I can't give it to you now."

"That's okay. Go on — open it."

Val carefully removed the wrapping paper, and gasped in delight when she saw what was inside. "It's Holly!" she cried, holding up the carved wooden figure of a deer. "It looks exactly like her! Did you make this yourself, Toby?"

Toby shook his head. "No. My older brother did. Luke's really good at woodcarving, so I gave him a picture I took of Holly a couple of weeks ago. I thought maybe you'd want to have something to remember her by after Doc takes her to Wildlife Farm."

Running a finger over the smooth, golden wood, Val beamed at him. "I love it," she said. "I'll keep it forever. You couldn't have given me anything I'd have liked more!"

Toby's ears were bright pink as he said, "Merry Christmas, Val."

"Merry Christmas, Toby."

Just then, she heard a series of chords on the piano, and Mayor Anderson's voice saying loudly, "Ladies and gentlemen, may I have your attention, please? I've just been informed by our hostess that Doctor Theodore Taylor and Catherine Sparks have something very important to tell us!"

Leaping up from her seat, Val grabbed Toby's hand and pulled him toward the living room. "Let's go," she cried. "This is one announcement I don't want to miss!"

Doc was standing by the grand piano, looking very handsome in his best suit, and very happy. Catherine, lovely and smiling in a green silk dress and pearls, was by his side. As Val and Toby entered, Catherine held out her hand.

"Please join us, Val," she said, and Doc motioned for Teddy, Erin, and Sparky to come over, too.

Val and Erin stood next to Catherine, and Teddy and Sparky, giggling self-consciously, stood beside Doc while the rest of Miss Maggie's guests gathered around them in expectant silence.

Doc glanced at Catherine, then cleared his throat. "What we have to say won't take long, and to many of you it won't come as a great surprise. But Catherine and I thought that this was the best possible time to inform all of you, our dear friends, that we decided . . ."

"I thought you said it wasn't going to take long," Teddy whispered loudly, tugging at his father's jacket.

"Yes, Ted." Catherine linked her arm through his. "Do come to the point so we can get back to the party!"

Smiling at the assembled guests, Doc said, "All right, here it is. You all know Catherine's family, and you all know mine. But what you *don't* all know is that in less than six months . . ."

"May fifteenth, to be exact," Catherine added.

"On May fifteenth, we'll all be one family, because Catherine has agreed to be my wife!"

Even over the applause and cheers, Val could hear the tinkling of Miss Maggie's bells. The old lady was clapping harder than anyone else.

"Excellent idea, young Theodore," she shouted. "Congratulations to all six of you!"

"Guess this means I'm gonna have to put on my good suit again in May, don't it, Doc?" Mike Strickler called out, and everyone laughed.

As their friends surrounded Catherine and Doc, congratulating them and shaking their hands, Teddy and Sparky headed for the buffet.

"We're starvin' like Marvin," Sparky cried.

"Hey, Miss Maggie," Teddy yelled, "some of your cats are eating the turkey!"

"Drat!" Miss Maggie strode toward the dining room, muttering, "It must be Antony and Cleopatra — their manners leave a lot to be desired."

The mayor began playing "Deck the Halls," and Erin turned to Val.

"A May wedding," she said dreamily. Her eyes were shining as brightly as the ornaments on Miss

Maggie's tree. "Won't that be lovely? Do you think Catherine will let us be bridesmaids?"

"I bet she will." Val smiled at her sister. "Merry Christmas, Erin!"

Erin gave her a big hug. "Merry Christmas, Vallie!"

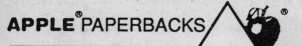

APPLE® PAPERBACKS

Pick an Apple and Polish Off Some Great Reading!

BEST-SELLING APPLE TITLES

❑ MT43944-8	**Afternoon of the Elves** Janet Taylor Lisle	$2.75
❑ MT43109-9	**Boys Are Yucko** Anna Grossnickle Hines	$2.95
❑ MT43473-X	**The Broccoli Tapes** Jan Slepian	$2.95
❑ MT40961-1	**Chocolate Covered Ants** Stephen Manes	$2.95
❑ MT45436-6	**Cousins** Virginia Hamilton	$2.95
❑ MT44036-5	**George Washington's Socks** Elvira Woodruff	$2.95
❑ MT45244-4	**Ghost Cadet** Elaine Marie Alphin	$2.95
❑ MT44351-8	**Help! I'm a Prisoner in the Library** Eth Clifford	$2.95
❑ MT43618-X	**Me and Katie (The Pest)** Ann M. Martin	$2.95
❑ MT43030-0	**Shoebag** Mary James	$2.95
❑ MT46075-7	**Sixth Grade Secrets** Louis Sachar	$2.95
❑ MT42882-9	**Sixth Grade Sleepover** Eve Bunting	$2.95
❑ MT41732-0	**Too Many Murphys** Colleen O'Shaughnessy McKenna	$2.95

Available wherever you buy books, or use this order form.

Scholastic Inc., P.O. Box 7502, 2931 East McCarty Street, Jefferson City, MO 65102

Please send me the books I have checked above. I am enclosing $_____ (please add $2.00 to cover shipping and handling). Send check or money order — no cash or C.O.D.s please.

Name_____ Birthdate_____

Address _____

City_____ State/Zip _____

Please allow four to six weeks for delivery. Offer good in the U.S.A. only. Sorry, mail orders are not available to residents of Canada. Prices subject to change.

APP693

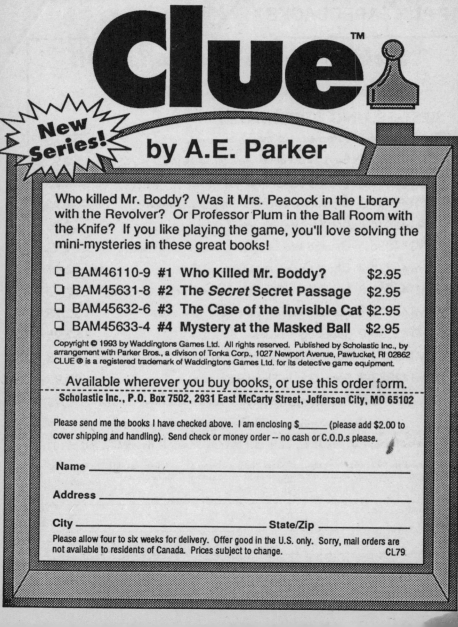

Get Goosebumps
by R.L. Stine
Now!